Deadly Dancing

Mars Cannon, Book 1

NICOLETTE PIERCE

For my Grandma Marie—
Thank you for stashing your "smut" books where I could find
them. You helped shape my future. I miss you every day.

Acknowledgments

An enormous thank you goes out to Nikki Gavin for giving me solid, spot-on advice. I couldn't have finished this book without you.

To Jaclyn Jacunski: Thank you for always having my back. Your support means the world to me.

Thank you to Frank Wassenberg for the new look of the Mars Cannon series. The cover is a great addition!

Aaron Dean, firefighter and writer, thank you for giving me a list of edits! The second edition is looking much better. I look forward to seeing your creative writing published.

Thank you to Amber Barry who helped with yet another round of editing. I appreciate your hard work and speedy turn around.

Books by Nicolette Pierce

Mars Cannon Novels
Deadly Dancing
Predator Patrol
Security Squad
Biker Brigade
Fearsome Foursome

Nadia Wolf Novels
The Big Blind
High Stakes
Cashing Out
Squeeze Play
The Last Tailored Suit
My Traitor
Pocketful of Diamonds
Last Hand

Metal Girls Novels
Melting Point
Critical Point
Breaking Point

Loved by Reese
When Rio Surrenders
When Rome Falls
When Edinburgh Dreams
When Sydney Loves
When London Calls

For more information, visit www.NicolettePierce.com.

Chapter 1

"We've got ourselves a big one this time!" a voice, shaky with age, shouted through a megaphone. "Code magenta!"

The voice jolted me awake. Code magenta? Oh, geez! It's Mrs. Janowski again. I dragged my face from the pillow and rolled over with a groan. My eyes cracked open to a narrow slit, allowing me to read the alarm clock. Ugh! It was six in the morning and on a Saturday, too. I buried my head under the pillow, but my legs had already made their way half off the bed. I crawled the rest of the way out, muttering curses.

I shuffled to the window and peered down to see Mrs. Janowski marching up and down the block, shouting battle cries through her husband's old army megaphone. She hadn't bothered getting dressed and was still wearing her fuzzy pink robe adorned with little blue flowers. The poufy pink tassels on her slippers bounced as she marched. Little curls of gray hair were mashed on one side of her head from sleep.

Mrs. Janowski was the sole neighborhood watchdog, and she took the self-appointed role very seriously. Ever since her husband died five years ago, she's been getting more vigilant in her eighty-plus years.

I sighed and trudged downstairs to the front door.

"Mrs. Janowski," I called to her from my doorstep, "what's going on?"

I didn't really want to know, but if it stopped her from yelling through that blasted megaphone, so be it. Plus, the neighbors were still ruffled from her last round with the megaphone.

"We just got word from headquarters that a mancer was found dead at Longhorn's Bar. It's looking like murder."

From previous experiences with Mrs. Janowski, I knew "headquarters" meant the police scanner she kept continuously turned on in her living room.

"What's a mancer?" I asked her through a yawn.

"It's a male exotic dancer," she replied with a shake of her head. "Isn't that something? Women paying men to shake their bobbles at them. I'm sure they would do it for free. Even Mr. Billick on the corner has given unsuspecting women free peeks. He's a spry thing."

My stomach churned. Mr. Billick had to be a hundred years old. He was the incredible shrinking man complete with a walker pimped out with tennis balls on its feet. I wouldn't consider him spry. Maybe I'd think differently if I was in my eighties like Mrs. Janowski.

"Did they say anything else about Longhorn's?" I asked. "I have an event there tonight."

"No, but the police and EMT are there now."

Great!

"By the way, what's 'code magenta'?"

"That's part of my new code system. Red is death, but entertainers need more pizzazz than just red. Magenta has pizzazz, doesn't it?"

I stared at her for a moment, trying to understand the logic, but at six in the morning, logic wasn't coming to me too quickly. "You could be right," I said to appease her. "I have to go and get ready."

"Me too. I have to get the new code system passed out to all the neighbors. Wouldn't want them to think code lime-green means a Jell-O party when it really means the roads are slimed."

Mrs. Janowski shuffled back to headquarters, and I returned home to shower. Of all the times there had to be a death, why today? I let the water pour over me until it turned icy cold. Slimy roads? I chuckled.

My name is Mars Cannon. My father, an astronomy teacher and enthusiast, gave me the nickname years ago and it stuck. He was never happy my mom named me Marsalla. It was my grandmother's name, and she always had a thorn in her side when it came to my dad.

My nickname may be odd, but my life isn't remotely odd or exciting. I'm able to describe myself as an average woman of thirty. I'd like to believe my two best features are my full lips and my almond-shaped blue eyes. I have shoulder-length hair that goes through various shades of brown. This time it happens to be golden chestnut. My downfall is my strawberries-and-cream complexion. My skin ordinarily tends toward cream, but the color of strawberries comes out when I'm overheated or embarrassed. Unfortunately, the latter happens way too often. I'm five feet and a handful of inches tall. I could stand to lose fifteen pounds or so. It all seems to reside in my chest, hips, and butt. It doesn't seem to make men run for the hills, so I don't get too worried about it. Of course, I haven't had a date in a while, so I may have to rethink that . . . but not now. I've been craving cheesecake . . . I always crave cheesecake.

My cell phone rang as I stepped out of the shower. I ran over to the nightstand to read Jocelyn's name on the caller ID. I cringed as I answered it.

"Hello?" I asked, knowing it was Jocelyn.

"I just heard on the news about the dead guy at Longhorn's," she said. "Go down there and do something."

"Do something?" I asked.

"Fix it!" she demanded. "I can't have a bachelorette party with no stage and no men." I heard her huff right before she hung up.

I work for Jocelyn McCain Events. Jocelyn and I have a long-standing arrangement in terms of my employment. Meaning, I work as many hours as needed to get the job done, and she lets me go about it with minimal interference—at least what she considers minimal.

Jocelyn is the face for Jocelyn McCain Events, but she doesn't want anything to do with the day-to-day operation. That's where I come in. She makes cameo appearances at events to schmooze the clients, leaving the details, setup, and cleanup in my hands. Most of the time, I work close to eighty hours and she works closer to ten. Since I'm salaried, my take-home pay is always the same and always dismal. It's enough money to get by, but not enough to have a life.

And I had every intention to "fix it." Tonight was an event, but it was also for my best friend, Kym.

I opened my bedroom window to let some fresh air in. The June air was already hot and humid. The perfect breeding ground for mosquitoes the size of melons. I made a mental note to stock up on sprays and citronella candles for our outdoor events.

I picked out a pale blue sundress with strings that tied around my neck and strappy sandals. I grabbed my purse as I headed out the door to find my twelve-year-old blue compact car waiting for me. It's a nice car, but it doesn't scream excitement or adventure. Reliability rarely screams anything at all.

I pulled into Longhorn's parking lot next to a squad car. There were only a couple of uniforms outside the building. An UrgentMed truck sat close to the door with Evan West sitting at the wheel. His window was rolled down as he waited.

Jocelyn McCain Events uses UrgentMed frequently for our larger events. You never know if someone will choke on a cocktail wiener or pass out from sunstroke. We try to avoid deaths and scenes of chaos by always being prepared. Evan worked with us on many occasions. Of course, that could be because I ask for him specifically, but I would never admit that to anyone. He's what a person might call "eye candy" . . . and I could really use a free sample.

"Mars." He smiled as I approached his window. "You always appear when I need a good tussle in the back of the truck. How about it?"

Evan was about as hot as they come. He had carefree dark hair that hung into his ice-blue eyes when he looked down at me from his five-eleven length. I figure he's about my age, but I've never asked. He's not overly muscular but deliciously firm and lean. His one great passion in life is to make women fall for him, and damn it was so easy.

If I didn't think about it, I would have jumped in back of his truck with him. Our relationship was that of a flirty nature. We've never dated nor been intimate. Mostly because he had girls falling over him and I don't like crowds. Evan liked to play with them and then put them aside to find a new one. He almost never circled back to a girl already conquered.

"Mmmm, you know I would love to, but I have business to take care of," I murmured as I pressed against the truck door to loop my finger around a curl by his neck. A flash of heat surged through me at the touch. I quickly unlooped my finger from his hair and pushed off the side of his truck. His arm shot through the window and wrapped around me, pressing me back into the door.

"The sundress you're wearing is sexy as hell," he rasped in my ear. "I'll be free soon. They're about ready to release the body and wrap things up here. My partner is in there now. Let me take you out later."

I gave him a lazy smile, which I was hoping had a bit of sexy to it, but it probably looked more like a nervous twitch. I unwrapped myself from his arms and floated, without another word, to the entrance of Longhorn's. That was a little too close. A few more minutes and I'd have been in the back of his truck with a satisfied smile on my face but with no hope of future flirting.

I reached the door and peeked in. The air in the bar was stale and it was darkly lit except for a couple of spotlights within the yellow-tape barricade near the stage. The police were still there, taking pictures and scribbling notes. The office was located on the opposite side of the bar. I decided I'd better go search in the office for the owner first.

A cop stepped in front of me to block my path. "Excuse me, this area is restricted. I'll have to ask you to leave."

"I just need to find the owner," I explained. "I have a party scheduled here tonight. I need to know if we're still on."

"You'll have to come by later and ask."

Later? My stomach flipped.

"I can't ask later," I explained. I moved closer, which forced me to stare up at the cop. I tried to keep my tone even and calm. "What if I can't have the party here? I'll have to find a different location. Do you know hard it is to find a place at the last minute?" I asked. I could feel my eye starting to twitch. "And then I'll have to notify everyone! What will I tell them?" By now, I'd worked myself up into a panic at having Kym's party ruined.

He stared down at me with a face of stone.

Pulling myself together quickly, I dug through my purse. "Here," I said. I pulled out my business card and pushed it into his hand. "Please make sure the owner calls me right away . . . er, Officer Dugan." I read his name tag, making a mental note to remember. "If I don't hear from him in an hour, I'll come back here looking for you." I gave him my best don't-mess-with-me stare just before he ushered me out the door and closed it behind me.

As I was escorted out, my eyes caught on a man on the other side of the road. He stood with his back leaned against the wall of a building and his muscular arms crossed in front of him. He stared straight at me with narrow eyes and a tightened jaw. I hadn't noticed him before because he'd fallen into the building's shadow . . . or it could have been because I was too focused on Evan. The man wore jeans and a dark-colored T-shirt. His short dark hair blended into a rugged few-day-old beard. He was probably a vision in the bedroom, but out here he scared the begeebers out of me. I couldn't see much else of him and that was fine with me.

I dropped into my car and took off. Within minutes my cell phone rang with the owner of Longhorn's telling me I could still have the party tonight. The crime scene was to be released by noon and a cleaning crew was already on their way. I smiled. I knew Officer Dugan liked me, even if he did kick me out.

By late afternoon, I was back at Longhorn's to get a lay of the land and to add a few tasteful decorations at our reserved tables. Well, as tasteful as decorations could be at a strip bar. A woman named Annie was there to let me in.

I looked around to see if any of the yellow tape remained. Most of it was gone except a small section at the back of the stage.

"Is this tape going to be here tonight?" I asked.

"Hard to say," she replied. "The owner didn't give me instructions on it. I was told the crime scene was released, so I wouldn't worry about it. I'll just hang a curtain in front of it; you'll never be able to see it."

"Thank you. That'd be wonderful," I said. "Do you mind if I ask who died?"

"No," she said. A small strand of her dark-blonde hair fell out of her ponytail. "It was Jesse Corbin. He liked to call himself Jesse James and used it as a stage name. I'm sorry he died, but he was a jerk."

I detected an exposed wound, so I treaded carefully.

"Do they know how he died?"

"The cops said he was hit with a sledgehammer," she said. Her hazel eyes focused on a glass she was polishing.

"A sledgehammer?" My stomach churned. "Do they have a suspect yet?"

She glanced warily at me. "You ask a lot of questions."

"I'm sorry. I overstepped," I said. "I have a natural tendency to be nosy. I get it from my mother." I shrugged my shoulders at a loss of what to say next.

She looked thoughtful for a moment. "I guess I'm a little anxious about the whole thing," she said. "They don't have a suspect yet."

Chapter 2

It was difficult deciding what to wear for the party. At typical business events I would wear a professional skirt suit or something business casual. Tonight, though, I could actually have fun and enjoy myself. There wouldn't be any reason to dress to impress clients. No men at the party to impress either except for the strippers, but they don't count.

I pulled on jeans and a loose-flowing, emerald-green shirt that was shoulderless and held in place by a ribbon tied around my neck. I pulled my hair into a ponytail and let a few hairs fall out to frame my face. I fluttered my eyelashes at the mascara wand and applied a light, glossy lipstick.

I created Kym's bachelorette party like I'd want for myself: a lot of friends and great food at The Lake Breeze restaurant. The male strip club, Longhorn's, which we will be heading to after, was added for Kym. It's not really my thing, but it's her party and she specifically requested it—or, rather, demanded.

There were nineteen girls and one feisty aunt at the bachelorette party. We dined out on the restaurant's patio overlooking the lake, drinking margaritas by the gallon. The hot, humid air formed beads of sweat on the glasses, but after the countless margaritas, no one seemed to notice the heat.

I kept a watchful eye over my friends, especially Kym. She, out of all of them, was the hardest to keep track of once she had a few too many. She was a happy drunk . . . way too happy. And there was no way to contain her colorful behavior once she began.

"Mars?" Kym asked, her blonde hair falling loose from a lopsided clip. "Will Jim and I be happy?"

I smiled at her. She already knew she'd be happy with him. And why wouldn't she be? He was handsome, rich, and worshipped her.

"You'll be very happy," I said.

Several of the other girls nodded their heads in agreement.

"You'll be so happy, you'll make all of us jealous," Kym's cousin said between her sips of margarita.

Once the noise level from our party went from talking to laughter and then to all-out-noisy celebration, it was time to head to Longhorn's.

I had hired four limos to be ready at a moment's notice for the night. The girls piled into the limos like boisterous, drunk circus clowns and tumbled out the same way when we arrived at the bar.

Being the only sober one, I was flushed and on edge with the task of herding the riot of cackling women into the bar. When we poured into the bar, the entertainment was already in full swing. They ogled and called out to the dancing men.

As I made my way to the bar to give Annie last-minute instructions, I peeked at the dancers as they removed dollars out of women's cleavage with their teeth. I was closing in on Annie when a flurry of hands grabbed my arms, waist, and legs. The girls hoisted me up and weaved their way to the catwalk.

"No!" I shouted. "Put me down this instant!" My frantic pleads were drowned by the heavy beat of dance music blasting from the speakers. I struggled to free myself.

They heaved me up to the stage, dropping me in front of a gyrating dancer whose manhood pulsed in his flimsy thong. Mrs. Janowski flashed through my mind, and I couldn't help but wonder what she'd think. I shook my head. This was not the time to think of Mrs. J. I looked up from the catwalk floor to see several men dancing their way closer to me. Their thongs stretched with dollar bills that fluttered as they moved. Their bulging muscles, slicked with oil, shimmered in the blinding stage lights.

My face colored red as one of the dancers approached me. I could hear some cat calls and whistles.

Kym, being the loudest, shouted to me, "Go on, Mars! Shake what you were born with!"

I ground my teeth. This was Kym's way of making me have a good time. I wouldn't say I'm a prude, but I don't get carried away at parties, and I'm always the designated driver. Plus, I will not dance with nearly naked men.

Tonight, my friends were having none of it, and I was going to suffer for it. Kym, the instigator, always wanted what was best for me, but our ideas about what's best for me are very different. I love her despite our gaping differences, but right now I wanted to leap off the stage and strangle her.

Having been here earlier to decorate, I remembered there was an exit off stage left. I quickly turned tail and ran, carefully avoiding contact with the virile dancers. One dancer, with a mop of blond hair and leopard-print thong, reached for me. I flew through the curtain.

Thud! I ran smack into a wall and landed on my behind.

"What the hell?" A tall, muscular man turned around to glance down at me.

My eyes snapped up to see him. It hadn't been a wall after all. The heat in my face elevated to near sun temperatures.

"Oh God, I'm so sorry!" I cringed. "I was coming from the stage and didn't see you. Are you okay?"

"A little thing like you can't hurt me." He smirked. "You're turning red."

I'm always red, but little? I guess compared to him I would be. He stood about six-two. His golden muscles rippled everywhere the eye could see, and I could see a lot considering he was only wearing a cowboy hat, boots, and a gold thong that stretched against his extremely nice bulge. He had his chaps in hand, ready to be put on before he hit the stage.

He pulled me onto my feet with little effort.

"Why are you back here?" he asked.

"Don't ask." I shook my head. "I'll just get out of your way."

He examined me for a moment with his warm, cocoa eyes. I gawked back in admiration of the view standing before me. I bit my lower lip to keep from licking my lips.

"Hungry?" he asked.

"What?"

"Sweet thing," he said smoothly, but without a drop of the Texas accent I had imagined. "You're looking at me like I'm the main entrée." His dark eyes crinkled on the verge of smiling.

"Um . . . no . . . I'm going to go." I turned on my heel to leave. His firm hand held my arm.

"I didn't mean to embarrass you. You can stay back here if you want, but in less than a minute, the dancers on stage are going to come back. You might become dessert if they see you." His hand traveled from my arm to my shoulder. His thumb traced my neck below my earlobe. Luscious heat waves traveled through my body at an alarming rate.

"Why would they want me? I heard most of the dancers are gay," Curtis, my coworker, had told me that. Now that I said it out loud, I had my doubts. It was probably just wishful thinking on his part.

"Uh, no," he replied with a laugh. "Some are and some aren't. The ones on set now definitely aren't. They'll have a little too much fun with you if they see you back here."

"Are you?" I asked before I could stop my words. I mentally kicked myself.

"You haven't figured it out yet?" He leaned in closer. "I'm more than happy to answer your question with a demonstration." A smile escaped the side of his mouth.

"I'm going back out front. I like my chances better out there."

"Good idea." He moved his hand off my shoulder.

I turned to leave. Damn, I really wouldn't have minded a demonstration from him.

"I'm on set next. Want me to dance for you?" he asked.

My mind raced and rendered me speechless. I made the most of my feet and fled.

Ugh! I didn't flirt or have a snappy comeback. He had me flustered and tongue-tied. I've failed womankind.

I found Kym not too far from the stage. She was staring at the other side of the room.

"There you are!" she scolded me. "I thought you might have ditched us after the stage bit. What took you so long back there?" Kym winked.

"I don't want to talk about it," I said. "What are you looking at?"

"You don't want to know."

I scanned the room and spotted her. Jocelyn was on the opposite side of the catwalk shaking her moneymakers at the blond dancer with the leopard-print thong. Dollars were pouring out of her hand and into the already-stretched thong. She had a backup supply of dollars that were wedged between her jumbo, silicone breasts.

The song ended and a new one thumped its thunderous bass beat. Out danced the cowboy from backstage and two other guys. My mouth swung open and I had to force myself to close it. Even though his frame was carved with hard muscles, he was agile on his feet. His movements peaked perfectly with the heart-thumping music. The lights played with his hard angles and lines.

"Oh, my God! He's hot!" Kym yelled over to me. "If I wasn't getting married, I'd be all over him."

I flushed as he ripped off his chaps to reveal the gold thong I had already had the privilege of seeing up close.

Kym raised her fist of dollars and hollered, "Come over here and shake it, Cowboy!"

His eyes flicked over to Kym. He started slowly dancing in her direction, picking up dollars along the way from drooling women. His eyes moved past Kym and registered me. A smile crept on his face.

He danced his way closer and closer. Kym shivered with energy, bursting to give him all of her money. He gave her a brief, uninterested dance while she wedged bills into his thong. His molten eyes were glued to mine.

Even though every hormone in my body was surging to pandemonium proportions, I was confident he wouldn't come my way since I didn't have money falling out of me like a broken ATM. In fact, the only money I had was a twenty-dollar bill that was earmarked for food. No man, no matter how gorgeous, was going to earn it tonight.

I blinked. He was in front of me in two strides.

"Still hungry?" he rasped into my ear. Raw electricity radiated from him.

I touched the corner of my mouth, praying I didn't just drool. Our eyes locked. Sheer nervous panic made me reach for the twenty crumpled in my pocket. I shoved it in the front of his thong, snapping the elastic against him. My fingers burned at the touch of his skin. My face flared red. I needed air, fast. I turned and fled from the bar and didn't look back. I didn't want to think about how he probably laughed at my fleeing escape.

I leaned against the outside wall. Breathing in the fresh air helped clear my head. I was still befuddled and hot from his touch but nothing a few days of self-loathing and a huge cheesecake wouldn't fix . . . a turtle cheesecake with extra chocolate sauce. I slapped my hand to my head. I'd have to take a rain check on the cheesecake. I just gave the cowboy my last twenty and payday was days away.

The sun had dipped long ago, taking the blistering summer air away and replacing it with a refreshing cool breeze that had just a hint of lake. I breathed it in, forcing myself to relax.

Next week, Kym will marry Jim. One more friend lost to marriage. My pool of single friends was starting to dwindle. Our friendships always ended the same—reduced to acquaintance status. Sure, they never mean to stray, but they do. The spouse takes priority, which he should, and then babies come next. In the blink of an eye, a year or more has gone by and I bump into them in the supermarket. Promises are made that we'll see each other real soon. It never happens.

I'll miss Kym the most. Her infectious, happy attitude always cheered me. There was never a dull moment with her around. What will my life be like without her?

Ugh! Shake it off. The party would be ending soon, and I needed to make sure the limos were ready to take everyone home. I also needed to take down all the party decorations. I'm sure the cowboy is done dancing by now. Hopefully I can finish my work quickly without becoming a sex-starved buffoon.

Jocelyn strutted out. "I'm going home now. I gave the last of my money to the dishy cowboy." She smiled deviously. "Get his phone number for me," she said as she threw her deep-red hair back behind her shoulder and swung into her silver BMW. "Tah, tah!"

Yeah, sure. I'll get his phone number. Better yet, why not pimp him out to all of my friends, too? I glared at the BMW as it rounded the corner and drove out of view. I don't know what dug itself under my collar, but I had a sneaking suspicion it was the cowboy smothered with a heaping scoop of Jocelyn.

A dark town car pulled slowly to the front of the building. The windows were tinted, but the back window was rolled down a couple of inches. Small wisps of curling smoke floated out. The end of the cigarette lit up two narrow eyes. I shivered. The creep factor set my nerves on alert. I quickly surmised that being inside with the cowboy was a whole lot safer than standing out here. As I reached the front door, the limos pulled up, and the dark car slowly moved on.

The final set had just ended. Kym was draped on a chair with her head slumped over on the cocktail table.

"Kym?" I lightly tapped her shoulder.

"Huh?"

"It's time to go home. Are you going to be okay?"

"Yeppers." She giggled. "Jimmy-pooh is waiting for me. He said he wants to make sure I get home okay. He really means he wants to make sure I'm alone." More giggles escaped.

I pulled Kym from the table. "Can you stand?"

"Sure. No problem," Kym slurred as she wiggled her way out of her shoes and stood up with a slight rocking motion.

By the time I deposited all the jovially inebriated women into the limos and gave the drivers the addresses, it was nearly forty-five minutes later. I had stuck a sticky note on each woman's shirt with my cell phone number so their significant others could text me when they arrived home safely. Of course, I wouldn't do that at a normal event I was coordinating, but it's different with friends. They don't call me mother hen for nothing.

I figured it would take me a half-hour to clean up the decorations. I don't mind event cleanup. You don't have to be fussy—just rip, tear, pull, and yank. Most of it gets tossed anyway. It's just that in the wee morning hours, I'd rather be in bed.

A warm breath tickled my neck as I pulled down glittery, pink streamers.

"Hey, sweet thing."

"OMIGOD!" I screamed, swinging around to find the cowboy. He was standing so close, finding an escape route was almost impossible.

He was now dressed in a gray T-shirt that tugged against his chest and biceps. His jeans were relaxed but had just the right amount of snugness to leave me breathless. He smelled like soap, spicy berries, and sandalwood. If I could nuzzle into his chest for all eternity, I'd die happy.

"I'm sorry. I didn't mean to frighten you," he said with a grin. "You're very easy to rattle."

"I am not," I said. "I'm just not used to men sneaking up on me."

"You need some help?" He looked around the bar.

"No, I'm almost finished."

He was still close. His arms enclosed around, pinning me to the wall. His abs were rock hard against me.

I cast a speculative glance over his face. I was startled to find he was the man I had seen earlier. He was the one standing across the street.

"I saw you earlier today, didn't I?"

"Mmm-hmm," he growled and nipped at my earlobe. "You were wearing a sundress that showed off your very fine curves."

I attempted to push him away, but I sabotaged my own efforts. The man was delicious, and he liked my ample curves! And, I was way overdue for a man. My mind argued with the rest of my body as he kissed my neck and shoulder. I wasn't quite sure if my mind or body would win. I wasn't ready to find out.

Annie was still around somewhere. I could call out for help, but I wasn't ready to put the encounter on ice yet. I'm weak, so sue me.

"I really need to finish here," I said.

"So do I, sweet thing." His lips curled with amusement.

Amusement . . . at my expense. He wasn't into my curves, he was toying with me. Dammit!

I shoved him back with all my strength, producing a tiny fraction of space. Enough to allow my escape and give him a firm kick to the shin.

"Ow!" He winced but recovered quickly. "You kicked me."

"That's what you get for messing around in my head," I said. "You can't toy with me. I'm not your sweet thing nor am I hungry for you!"

Cowboy gazed down at me. A smile formed on his face. He raised his hands to signal a truce.

A sigh escaped my lips. "If you want to help, then take down the banners at the door; they're too high for me to reach. Otherwise, go away or I'll kick you again."

"You win this round. I'll help you take down the banners, and I won't try anything." He looked me in the eye and leaned in closer. "But the next round is mine."

A delightful shiver ran through me. Cowboy sauntered over to the banners and ripped them down.

"What's your name? Or should I just call you Cowboy?" I asked.

"It's Levi Mann."

"I'm Mars Cannon."

"Yeah, I know who you are," he said.

"How do you know who I am?"

"I make it my business to know." He grinned.

I looked at him with disbelief but shrugged it off. I'm not sure if I really wanted to know anyway.

"I guess it's nice to meet you," I said.

Actually, it was nice to meet him. He puzzled me. Not many men would stay to help me take down decorations after I'd kicked them. He had a relaxed, easygoing way about him when he wasn't trying to mess with my head. His eyes were soft and his smile was wider, more genuine.

We kept quiet, concentrating on getting the job done. With the two of us working at it, we were done in about fifteen minutes. We said goodnight to Annie, who was still cleaning up behind the bar, and exited out the back door to the parking lot.

The night air had dropped to a chilly temperature and the wind had picked up. I was freezing in my flimsy shirt. He wrapped his arm around my shoulders, keeping me warm.

I had to admit that walking next to Levi was nice. I usually walk by myself after an event or with one of the other coordinators, but they didn't make me feel safe. Emmy was known as a fainter, and Curtis squeals at the sight of spiders. With Levi, I somehow understood I was safe.

"Thank you for helping," I said quietly, not wanting to make eye contact.

Levi stopped and turned me to face him. His hand cupped my chin to lift my face toward his. "I was happy to," he said softly. His mouth closed in on mine. Fire rampaged from my stomach and raced through my body. His tongue teased my lips until I couldn't think of anything except wanting more. I parted to allow him in. He took advantage instantly. I let out a soft moan as he explored, playing with my tongue. My arms wrapped around his neck, and he pulled me in closer. I was dripping with need for him—and he knew it.

He stepped back suddenly. His white teeth were framed by his playful smile. "Round two is mine."

"No way," I said, still wanting more and befuddled from his touch. "That wasn't yours. I let you kiss me."

Levi grinned and steered me to my car. He took my keys from my hand and unlocked the door, only handing them back in exchange for a smaller but equally tantalizing kiss. He helped me in, shut the door, and watched me pull away. Was I just dismissed? I tried to look back from my rearview mirror but he was already out of sight.

I didn't think to offer my phone number. I'm not sure I'd have given it to him even if he'd asked for it. Why didn't he ask for it? I'm better off this way. Remaining strangers is better . . . if only I could make myself believe it.

He was too smooth and yummy for my blood. I'm sure he took advantage of all the girls who ambled through those club doors. I was just another fly intrigued by his well-endowed web.

I pulled into my driveway and slipped into my house. As I closed the door, I spotted a dark town car sitting across the street.

Chapter 3

I was too tired from the party to dream of Levi, but he must have drifted in there a couple of times because I woke up exhausted and frustrated. The morning sun poured into my windows, stirring me awake at ten.

I had my Sunday routine down to a science: sleep in, go to lunch with my mom, go grocery shopping, pick up a movie, curl up on the couch and watch the movie, and then go to sleep. Even though I was tired, I didn't see any reason for me to change this routine.

I showered and applied the tiniest bit of makeup. Just enough to remove the dark, Levi-induced circles from my eyes and brighten my complexion.

If I hurried, I could grab a caramel macchiato before meeting Mom. I needed the extra jolt before going rounds with her. She and I are similar in a lot of physical ways, but our ideas are completely opposite. "Get a husband before they are all gone," she lectures me. Yeah, I'll just pick the next guy off the street.

Levi flashed through my mind. I couldn't see bringing Levi home to my parents. I'd be mortally embarrassed to tell them he was a sexy exotic dancer. I could leave off the sexy part; it's obvious. I also couldn't see Levi being the marrying type. His career choice screamed bachelor. No strings or ties were going to snag him and get him to settle down.

I found my way to Capital Coffee with thirty minutes to spare. I shoved my hand into the car seats and dug around to find enough change, along with a crinkled dollar bill in the cup holder, to buy my macchiato.

I placed my order with a perky high school girl. She handed me my coffee and said, "Thank you, ma'am. Come again."

I hate when they call me ma'am, but I sipped my coffee and let it roll off by back. Its delightful warmth spread through me. It's my happy juice and gets me through the day. I read somewhere that caffeine is a drug. If it's true, then get me to rehab.

I stared out the window to watch people come and go. Capital Coffee is located in downtown Madison, Wisconsin, and is a melting pot of young university students, old politicians, and everything in between. I love it here because, even though it's a small city, there are so many wonderful things about it. Students can be found everywhere. Studying on blankets in the park and milling around near the university. Sparkling lakes surround the city, and hip boutique stores dot the streets.

My eyes drifted to the far side of the street. A black town car idled there. The back window was rolled down a few inches. It looked similar to the town car I had seen at the club. I couldn't see in, but I had the icky sensation someone was watching me.

I peeked at my watch. It was time to meet Mom at Rosalina's Café. Rosalina's was only a couple of blocks away. I left my car at Capital Coffee and walked down the street. I cut across, making sure to stay far away from the town car.

I caught a glimpse of my mom at a table on the sidewalk patio. She looked relaxed with a zinfandel in her hand. A large pink flower that matched her dress and heels was attached to an oversized black sunhat. Her dark-blonde hair was pulled back into a small bun at the nape of her neck. Sunglasses slid down her nose while she read the menu. Her thin bracelets gathered and clinked on her wrist.

My parents have been separated since I left home. I'm not sure the reason, but I'm pretty sure they drifted apart. When I left, so did their one big reason to remain together. I believe deep down they still love each other, otherwise they'd have divorced by now. I have a childish dream that they'll get back together.

"Hi, Mom."

"Oh, there you are, sweetheart," she said, motioning for me to sit down. "I've been trying to decide what to order, and I can't seem to choose anything. Should I go healthy with a garden salad or be naughty and order a stuffed panini with fries?"

"How about ordering a panini with a garden salad?"

"I guess it'd be a good compromise, but I've been longing for fries." She snapped the menu shut. "That settles it; I'll get the panini and fries."

"You can be naughty and get the fries. I'll be good and get the salad. We'll balance each other out."

A stressed-out waitress took our order and hurried off.

Mom glanced at me. "That's your problem, you know."

"What's my problem?"

"You're always being too safe and never enjoying life," she said. "I'm always afraid you'll end up marrying a stuffy tax accountant and having whiney children—or worse, ending up alone." She paused, most likely envisioning her future whiney grandchildren. "Have you been seeing anyone?"

We've arrived at the topic sooner than expected. It normally takes her two glasses of wine before she wears me down with questions about my love life . . . or lack thereof.

"Mom, you know I'm busy," I said. "We always have this talk and it's always the same."

She looked pained, so I threw her a bone. "I did meet someone last night. He is extremely cute and has a well-paying job."

I looked to the sky for a lightning bolt to strike me dead. For centuries, daughters have learned to edit what they tell their mothers. I'm just following in their hallowed footsteps.

Her blue eyes sparkled. "Oh, honey! I'm so excited." And she was excited. Her face lit up and she smiled as if the man had proposed.

"When can I meet him?"

"Uh, well, he's very busy at work, and I just met him. You'll have to give me time."

"Time for what? We can't let him get away, can we?"

I looked down at the salad the waitress placed in front of me and stabbed an unsuspecting carrot with my fork.

* * *

After my narrow escape at lunch and my empty pocketbook, I skipped the supermarket and decided to go home. I had to clean the closets anyway. And for entertainment tonight there's a free movie on the romance channel. Oh, God! My mom's right; I am safe and boring!

I plopped into my car and noticed a note stuck on my windshield. I leaned out, yanking it free from the wipers.

Keep your hands off him or you'll regret it!

Keep my hands off who? Is this supposed to be on my car or someone else's? Perhaps the perky coffee girl was supposed to get this.

Who am I supposed to leave alone? Levi? I just met him, and no one would have known. It could be Evan, but I've never even kissed him. An image of Evan's lips on mine flashed through my mind and sent an instant shiver through me. I shook it out of my head.

This is stupid! I crumpled up the note, tossed it in my back seat, and drove home.

*   *   *

My house is located on a street lined with skinny houses. It looks like an unnatural force slammed a bunch of houses together and mine landed smack-dab in the middle. It's two stories painted white with yellow trim and is almost as narrow as an alley. A living room and kitchen take up the entire first floor. The second floor holds my bedroom and a small bathroom.

My living room window has a flower box, which I enjoy. I'm not a gardener by any means, but I do appreciate brightly colored flowers outside my window in the summer. The inside of my house is "cozy," which is real-estate-agent lingo for microscopic. The walls were painted by the previous occupants, and I had never attempted to repaint. The color choices are a bit dubious with burnt oranges and various shades of green. I've done my best to color correct with the triple Ps: pictures, pillows, and plants. I'm sure it's hideous, but I'm in denial.

My furniture is old, bordering on decrepit. I like to think of it as "comfortable." There's still plenty of wear left, and it's nicely broken in. And no matter what you're looking for, there's a good chance it's stuck in the cushions somewhere.

Kym passed through my thoughts. I cringed at the hangover she must be experiencing. I reached into my pocket for my cell phone, but when I didn't find it, I realized I must have left it my car.

I ran back to the car and dug around. I found the phone under the driver's seat next to some dust bunnies and a fossilized French fry. I turned on the phone and scrolled through my contacts for Kym. Shutting the car door, I turned back to the house and walked straight into a Jolly Green Giant-sized man with a tarantula tattoo on his neck. I gasped and my eyes shot up to his face. He didn't look friendly like the Jolly Green Giant. He firmly took hold of my upper arm with his big meaty hands, pulling me to a black town car parked only a few feet away.

He held me close to the back window. My stomach churned. This guy was bad news. I couldn't see anything through the cracked window, but a low voice came from the back seat. "Where is he?"

"Where is who?" I squeaked. Stay calm, I told myself. Whatever you do, don't cry, faint, or mess your pants.

I'm going to die!

"The man you were with last night."

"The only man I was with last night was Levi, but I don't know him. I had just met him at the club. You should go back there and find out where he is."

"I consider myself a patient man. I'll be back soon. Tell him I want what's mine, or I'll take something of his."

"But I don't know him," I said.

"You better, or I might find myself becoming impatient. A pretty girl like you would make an excellent bargaining chip," he sneered. "If I don't get what I want, I'll come back for you. I know just what to do with you."

As the window rolled up, the tarantula goon released me with a shove. I watched as he angled into the driver's seat and drove away. I stood there in stunned silence. What just happened?

I had to find Levi, but the club was closed on Sundays. Did this have anything to do with the note? The note said to leave him alone, but this guy is telling me to find him.

Now what? Should I call the cops? And tell them what? I didn't even get the license plate number. I bolted back into the house and locked the door. I waited for my breathing to come back down to normal.

I held out my phone and steadied my hand long enough to dial Kym's number.

"'ello?" Kym slurred into the phone.

I winced at the pain in her voice. She was in no shape to help me. "Are you okay, Kym?"

"I'm going to die!" she cried into the phone.

"Should I let you go?"

"No, you have to tell me about the sexy cowboy. I don't remember the whole evening, but I do remember the way he looked at you."

"I don't know what you're talking about."

"Liar. Did you get his name? Something happened. I can feel it."

"It's probably just the hangover," I said.

"Fine, if you don't want to tell me then I'm going back to bed. But just so you know, if a guy looked at me the way the cowboy looked at you, I'd snatch him up and have my way with him. Guys like him are a rare find. Use him 'til he's ragged but still begging for more." She half-heartedly giggled before she groaned, threw up, and then hung up.

I grimaced at my phone after she threw up. She didn't give me bad advice. Unfortunately, it'd happen the other way around. I'd be ragged and begging while he fled to a different bed.

I wanted to tell someone what had happened, but who could do anything about it? I'd have to wait until tomorrow to call Longhorn's and find Levi. He can deal with it, and if not, then I'll go to the police.

I shoved Levi and the scary town car guys out of my mind, turned on the TV, and cuddled into my couch with a steaming mug of hot chocolate. Chocolate makes the world a better place . . . even if it did come from an ancient package from the back of my cupboard.

Chapter 4

Monday morning arrived too soon, and I was running in panic mode. The wedding was five days away, and I had last-minute details to iron out. Not to mention a slew of events were looming in the very near future.

I ran into the office and plunked down at my haphazardly organized desk. Emmy breezed by, setting files on my desk.

Emmy is the receptionist and helps with events if we need extra hands. She's in her mid-twenties and is sweet and friendly. Her demeanor sometimes gives way to spurts of flightiness, but she is otherwise dependable and a hard worker.

"Jocelyn wants you to start working on two new events. One is for this Friday night."

"What?" I asked. "I can't work Friday. I have the wedding rehearsal dinner that night. I told her I couldn't work Friday or Saturday."

"I hear you, but she's in a mood. If you talk to her, watch out."

Jocelyn is always in a mood, especially on Monday mornings. I like to imagine it's because, even with all her prowling around during the weekend, she never captures her prey.

I worked up the courage and marched into her office.

"Don't you knock?" Her eyebrow arched and her puffed-up lips tightened together . . . as much as they could.

"I need to talk to you about the Stevenson dinner on Friday. I can't work it. I have the wedding rehearsal dinner to go to."

"I'm not concerned about your plans. Just get the job done," she said.

"I've already been approved for vacation on Friday and Saturday. Not to mention, Kym is a paying client."

Jocelyn sighed dramatically, tapping her long red fingernails on her desk. "You're going to make a thing about this, aren't you?"

"You know I'd work this event if I didn't already have plans."

"Fine," she huffed. "I'll make you a deal: you take charge of organizing the event, and Curtis and Emmy can cover it."

"Deal," I said and turned to the door.

"Oh," she said before I could escape, "I almost forgot to ask what that guy's phone number is."

"Whose phone number?"

"That sexy beast of a man from the club. I told you to get his phone number."

"I thought you were kidding."

"I never joke about men," she said, tossing her hair over her shoulder.

"I have to make a phone call to Longhorn's today. I'll see if anyone knows."

Jocelyn's eyes perked. "Tell me as soon as you get off the phone."

"Sure."

I looked down at the Stevenson file in my hand. My heart contracted. Why did I agree to this?

I sat at my desk. It won't be too bad, I reassured myself. Just one more task on my never-ending list of things to do. I opened the file and took out the request form Emmy had the Stevensons fill out.

Pressure dissipated as I read the form. The Stevenson dinner should be a breeze. It's for their fiftieth wedding anniversary and looked like a meat-and-potatoes type of family get-together. Throw in some candles, music, and flowers, and you've got yourself a nice party. Of course, I say that now, but I'm known to try to wiggle in extra touches to make the event more memorable. It drives Jocelyn wild. "You can't just give things away; we have bills to pay," she'd say. Yeah, bills for her Botox and plastic surgery.

I handed the file off to Curtis with a scribbled list of arrangements. He could start working on the arrangements while I concentrated on the wedding. He was used to deciphering my notes.

"What is this?" He held my list between his fingers as if it could turn into a poisonous snake at any moment.

"It's for the Stevenson party on Friday night."

"Friday night? When did this come in?"

"I don't know. Emmy just gave me the file."

I returned to my desk to call Longhorn's. I had to reach Levi. He was going to get involved in this mess whether he wanted to or not.

I flipped through my business cards until I found the club's number. I dialed and heard a woman's voice on the other end.

"Longhorn's," she said.

"Hi, I'm trying to locate one of your dancers. I was hoping you could help me."

"Honey, it was just one night. Move on. I'm sure you've had a one-night stand before, and if not, hey, it's a new experience with a hot guy. You aren't pregnant are you?" she asked with a monotone voice that's heard it all before.

Oh, my!

"No, it's not like that." I said. "My name is Mars Cannon. I'm the events coordinator that had the bachelorette party Saturday night. I'm looking for Levi Mann. I have a message from . . . well, I'm not sure who it's from. But they are searching for him, and I'm somehow stuck in the middle."

"Oh, Mars, it's Annie. I didn't mean to lecture you on one-night stands," she said. "We get all sorts of calls from women who believe they found the perfect someone only to find out he's just another jerk. The guys are all jerks here. They think they're God's gift to women just because they're good-looking. I don't know what women think when they come here. It's not like we're a match-making business. We're more like a fool's paradise."

"I understand. It's just that I seem to find myself in a situation, and I need Levi to straighten it out."

"I'm not sure who Levi is. Can you describe him?"

"He was dressed as a cowboy. He helped me take down the decorations after."

"Oh, that's Nick Heat. He's always switching his stage name. He's such a looker that the ladies like to harass him during his off time."

Levi Mann and Nick Heat? I'm such a sucker. I really believed his name was Levi. He must think I'm the dumbest sap there is.

"Can you give me his phone number?"

"Sorry, hon, I can't because it's against company policy. How about if you give me your number, and I'll call him with your message?"

"Okay, that's fine. Just out of curiosity, how long has Levi . . . er, Nick worked for you?" I asked.

"He started with us a few months back." She gave a low, throaty laugh. "I remember his first day on the job. He was white as a sheet when he came from behind the curtain and out onto the catwalk. By his second number, he was getting the most tips."

I gave her my number, thanked her for her time, and hung up.

So, Levi is not Levi but possibly Nick instead. I puffed out a breath. I had a feeling I might need to keep a journal of the growing number of stage names. No, because once I get this all straightened out, he'll be out of my life.

I guess I can understand the need for a stage name to protect his identity. It irked me, though. I don't like getting lied to. There was something about Levi-Nick. I'm not sure how exotic dancers normally act, but he sensed things. He was aware of himself and his surroundings.

I reached for my phone to call the florist with an order just as my phone extension rang.

"Mars Cannon. How may I help you?" I asked.

"Hungry?" Levi-Nick purred.

An instant flash of heat sizzled through me as I recognized his voice. "Don't start that again!"

He chuckled. "Actually, I want to take you out to dinner tonight."

I thought about the offer. I was going to starve otherwise. My cupboards were bare, and he did take my last twenty dollars. Okay, he didn't take it. But he made me momentarily daffy, and I gave him the twenty. So, in essence, he did take it.

"Are you still there?" he asked.

"Yes, I was just thinking."

"Can't trust yourself to keep your hands off me, can you?"

"Don't worry about my hands, worry about your own," I retorted. "I'll go to dinner if you tell me your real name. Annie told me your name was Nick."

"When did you talk to her?"

"A few minutes before you called," I said. "I told her to give you a message. Didn't you get it?"

"No." He sounded confused.

"Oh, she must not have phoned you in time. How did you know to call me?"

"I was dreaming about you and your soft, full lips all day yesterday. Did you think I'd let you leave after our little kiss without getting your information?"

"I sure as heck didn't give you my phone number."

"A minor technicality," he said. "When should I pick you up?"

I wasn't about to give him my address. "I'll meet you at For Pete's Sake at six."

"Don't trust me to take you home, huh?"

"I trust you'd take me home, but I don't trust that I could get you to leave," I said and hung up.

Damn, I still didn't know his name, and I didn't tell him about the creepy town car guys.

* * *

I worked steadily until knots formed in my neck. I hated working behind a desk, but some work required one. I stood and grabbed my purse. I'll head down to the florist instead of calling in my order. It'd be nice to see the flowers anyway. Flowers make me happy. What can I say? I'm a simple woman with simple needs.

I drove my car to Flower Power. I've driven there so many times my car was nearly on automatic pilot. I normally send my business to them because they're creative and always have fresh, beautiful flowers.

It's been owned by a mother and daughter for decades. The mother, Gloria, is in her seventies and is an original flower child from the sixties. She has long silver hair that she braids with flowers. She wears colorful, flowing clothes. Even though she has remained a flower child her whole life, she doesn't seem stuck in the past, just accentuated by it.

Her daughter, Willow, doesn't have the loud wardrobe or demeanor of her mother. She has a wistful way about her that calms even the most agitated client. The grandson, Kirby, is the delivery driver. His favorite hobby is getting stoned—Kirby excels at that.

"Mars!" Gloria exclaimed. "I always love when you come to visit us. Willow," she called to the back room. "Mars is here. Bring her some tea. We can sit down and chat."

Gloria's hair was decorated with dandelions today. She looked like a cute little grandma in a time warp. Her love beads rattled together as she shuffled to the back.

"Willow, are you there?" she asked. When there wasn't an answer, Gloria pondered for a moment. A spark of realization lit up her face. "Doggone, I forgot she left for the flower wholesale market today. We'll have to get along without her."

Gloria shuffled to the back room and poured two cups of herbal tea. She carefully handed me a cup, and we took a seat at a rickety round table painted yellow with a kaleidoscope of iridescent colors swirling together. Books were scattered about, mostly titles about flowers.

I picked one up and leafed through it, trying to get ideas. I needed flowers for the Madison Ladies' luncheon that was being held next week. These ladies had serious money, but they also had nimble fingers that liked to take home any trinkets they could get their hands on. I stopped on a page with bright gerbera daisies that would be perfect for fun wristlets. I could attach them to rolled cloth napkins. The ladies could wear them and take them home at the end of the event.

I pointed to the picture in the book. "I want these daisies made into wristlets."

"Great, I'll see if we can get those at the market," she said. "How many do you need?"

"There are thirty-four ladies. So, why don't you give me thirty-eight to be on the safe side."

"Far out," she said, not as an exclamation but more as an acknowledgement.

"I'll also need flowers for a dinner on Friday."

"So soon?"

"Yes, I just found out about it. It's for seventy-five guests. Just make fourteen centerpieces for the tables. Whatever flowers you can get by then will be fine."

"Sure, I can dig it," she said.

I suppressed a smile. She might have been a hip, groovy lady in her time, but now she was just adorable. If I had any auntie skills, I'd have pinched her cheeks.

"Willow and Kirby will be sorry to have missed you," she said as I stood to leave.

"Give them my best. I'm sure I'll be back soon. I always see Kirby for delivery of the flowers."

"Kirby says you're 'heavy.'"

"Ah, okay. Tell him thanks," I said, stepping outside with a little wave to Gloria. Did I just get insulted or complimented? I smiled. It didn't matter. Someday I will have to ask Gloria more about her past.

My next stop was the jewelry store. Jonathan's going to throw darts at me when I tell him what I want.

I pulled in front of the store and hopped out. Through the store window I could see Mr. Jonathan Alexander cleaning the cases. He looked at me with a smile; dollar signs registered in eyes.

"Mars!" he cried as I walked in the door. "I've missed you. Tell me you're here to buy some ridiculous amount of expensive jewelry."

"Yes, but don't go crazy on the expensive part."

"Do tell," he said, clasping his hands together with excitement.

"I'm here to buy seventy-five heart-shaped lockets, but I need them by Thursday for a dinner on Friday."

His jaw dropped and his hands fell to his side.

"Mars, I can't get an order here that fast," he said.

"I would have given you more time, but I just found out about the party today."

"If I had another week, I could do it for sure."

"I know," I said. "Listen, try your best to get them to me by Thursday with an engraving on each one, and I'll make sure everyone knows they came from your store."

His eyes dilated and his hands clasped together again. "I can't make any promises," he said.

I handed him a piece of notepaper with the engraving detail. I'd have to call the Stevensons' children to find old photos of the anniversary couple so they can be placed into the lockets.

It'd be a royal pain in the behind, but I get mushy when it comes to people in love, especially if they've been married for half of a century. It's the type of life most people dream about. Finding that special someone and living a lifetime together; it's a beautiful thing.

My stomach growled. I put my hand on it to quiet it down. I needed food. I had no money and my only credit card was maxed out so I couldn't even use that. I should've asked for an advance on my pay, but then Jocelyn would have scoffed at me and made a big deal about how she was saving me from starvation. I'd rather starve.

* * *

My cell phone rang as I pulled into my driveway.

"Hi, Mars," Kym said.

"How are you feeling?"

"I'm alive, but I'm still suffering the side effects. It was worth it, though. From what I can remember, I had fun."

"From what I can remember, you had way too much fun."

She laughed. "I wanted to make sure you remember to go to the bridal shop tomorrow for your final fitting. It's at two o'clock; don't be late."

"It's on my calendar. I promise I won't miss it," I reassured her.

"Good. And remember, you said you'd come over to my house afterward so we can work on the wedding favors."

"Of course!" I said with a little too much enthusiasm. I actually had forgotten. Kym knows me too well; it's scary. Why she picked me for maid of honor, I have no idea. I wouldn't even want me for a maid of honor.

"So, tell me something new," she said.

"Well, I'm going on a date tonight and, unless I'm delusional, I'm being stalked and threatened by one or possibly two different people."

"Oh, this is going to be good. Tell me everything and don't leave out details!"

"Well, two guys seem to be looking for that dancer from Saturday. He told me his name was Levi, but now I've been told it's Nick. He called me today and wants to have dinner." I thought back. "Yesterday, I found a note on my car to stay away from him. I'm assuming it meant Nick. The only other person who's taken an interest in me is Evan, but that's harmless flirting."

"Oh, I'm all tingly. It's like a James Bond film!"

"It's not like a James Bond film at all. You can trade places with me any day."

"We'll have to try that someday." She giggled. "But you should be careful. I wouldn't say it's harmless flirting with Evan. There are a lot of girls head over heels for him. I'm sure they'd tell you to back off their man."

"I see the guy occasionally at events. We flirt, but that's it. There's never any physical contact." Well, that had been the case until he pulled me against his truck on Saturday.

"I know it and you know it, but they don't know it. It's almost a game for Evan, and it's going to bite him in the ass. I'm sure he has plenty of women looking to get even, and some may be under the impression he is exclusive with them."

"Evan doesn't ever give the impression of being exclusive. From what I've witnessed, women are well aware of his stance. If it is about Evan, it shouldn't be a problem. I don't have any events with him until next month. Hopefully, everything will cool down by then."

"I hope so," she said.

We hung up, and I stared into my closet, contemplating what to wear tonight. Men have it so easy. Levi-Nick can reach into his closet and pull out a shirt or pants at random and they'd probably be perfect. Women have to slave over their wardrobe, hair, and makeup.

I picked out a little red dress that fit snuggly on top and had a bouncy short skirt. I pulled out my red three-inch heels.

I had no idea what to do with my hair. The change in the weather was making my normally straight hair curl into frizzy corkscrews. I pulled it up and gathered it in a clip, adding a few bobby pins to hold it in place. A few curls let loose right away. I applied a small amount of makeup. Done.

My stomach fluttered. I wasn't sure if it was because of hunger or Nick.

I grabbed a sheer black scarf in case I needed a layer around my shoulders later. I imagined Nick's hands on my shoulders instead and flushed. I'd definitely prefer his hands to a scarf.

I snatched my keys from the end table and headed out.

Mrs. Janowski was outside on her porch. Her hands were tightly wrapped around a large pair of binoculars that she was spying through.

"Hi, Mars! Looks like you have a humdinger of a date tonight."

"Yes," I called to her. "I'm heading out now."

"Have a good time, dear. And don't worry about a thing. I have the street under surveillance tonight."

Bad guys beware!

Chapter 5

Nick was leaned up against the side of the building waiting for me.

"You look surly when you lean against walls," I said.

Nick gazed at me with carnivorous eyes that made me afraid he could see right through my clothes. "I only look that way because I was wondering what I'd do if you stood me up."

"I don't believe you for a second. You looked that way on Saturday, too," I said. "I'm only a few minutes late."

"The longest few minutes of my life," he said as he looked into my eyes and did an appreciative glance downward. He took a curl from my hair and gently touched it.

"Should we go in?" he asked.

"Yes, I'm starving."

We strolled into For Pete's Sake. It's a modern restaurant with a throwback to a Bohemian style. My friends Pete and Angela owned it. They were high school sweethearts and had taken culinary classes together through college. I reasoned that if I brought Nick here and he turned into a creep, I'd have friends to turn to.

"Mars!" Angela exclaimed. "I didn't know you were coming in tonight."

"I'm sorry I didn't call. Can you squeeze us in?"

"Of course I can. What kind of friend would I be if I didn't?" She smiled and took a peek over my shoulder at Nick. "Party of two, I see," she said.

"Yes," I hissed in her ear. "And keep it on the down low."

"Hmpf," she responded. "Right this way."

Nick and I followed her through the restaurant until we stood in front of a teeny-tiny couple's booth that was slightly secluded from the main dining room.

"Is this all you have?" I nudged her.

"You didn't make a reservation, and this is all I have," she said.

I scanned the restaurant to see a dozen empty tables. I slid a narrow eye to her.

"This is perfect," Nick said.

I looked at him then at Angela. My face bloomed.

"I'll leave you two alone." Angela smirked and ran off.

"Will you fit in this booth?" I asked.

"We'll see."

It took a little maneuvering, but we were able to wedge in. His long legs took up all the space under the table, so he pulled my legs on top of his lap.

"This is ridiculous," I said, fidgeting in my seat. "Angela did this on purpose."

"She's my new favorite person."

"We can go somewhere else, or I can find Pete and he'll move us."

"Don't you dare," he said.

I huffed and squirmed until I positioned myself so I was at least a little more comfortable. Nick just sat back calmly. It didn't seem like anything could bother him.

He slipped the shoes off my feet, letting them fall to the floor. My stomach plummeted with the shoes.

"What are you doing?" I asked.

"You seem tense."

His thumb dug into a pressure point in the instep of my foot. God, his hands were like magic. My insides turned to goo. I gradually relaxed.

"Hi-yah!" Pete called as he walked over.

At the sound of his voice, my knee jarred, crashing into the underside of the table.

"Ow," I whimpered and rubbed my knee.

"I didn't know you were coming to see us tonight," Pete said.

Pete was dressed in his chef uniform and looked a little disheveled from working in the kitchen, but not nearly disheveled as I was at the moment.

"Whoa, what's this? Did Angela put you here?" His eyebrow arched.

I gave him a look that told him he was the biggest moron. "What do you think?"

He gave a knowing nod. "I'd tell you to move to a different table, but Angela would kill me. She loves it when she can stuff people back here. She's all into matchmaking right now," he said. "You can move to a different table, but it didn't come from me. I'll deny ever saying it."

"We're stuck in here now. Just make sure we aren't still here when you close up," I said.

"Sure." He nodded and gave me a friendly kiss on the cheek. He extended his hand to Nick. "I'm Pete."

"Nice to meet you," Nick said, shaking his hand. "I'm Chance."

Pete's face lit up and he snapped his fingers. "A-ha! I know just what I'm going to make for you two." Pete turned and left for the kitchen.

"I take it we don't order food here," Nick said.

"Chance?"

"What?" He grinned. "It's not a bad name. I use it onstage sometimes. Chance Encounters has a ring to it. Kind of like destiny."

"That's it! If you can't tell me your real name, then you're not worth my time."

I tried to move my feet wedged between his legs and the table. The man with three names sat contently, watching me struggle. I twisted my body to pull myself out. His hands wrapped around my waist, bringing me back before I could free myself.

"Calm down. Just hear me out before you run off."

I narrowed my eyes at him and crossed my arms.

"Don't pout. It makes you look irresistible."

"I'm not pouting," I said. Okay, I was pouting, dammit.

"Listen," Nick drew my hand across the table, "there are some circumstances preventing me from telling you. I'm not trying to be a jerk, but I really can't tell you."

I made a move to leave again.

"Wait," he sighed, "I can see this is going to be a problem for you. All I'm asking is that you trust me for the rest of the week. I should be able to tell you by then."

I eyed him suspiciously. "What am I supposed to call you?" I asked. "I now have three names for you, and I don't like any of them."

"Make up a name for me, and I'll go by that name." He paused. "But be nice. I don't want to be called Shirley or something like that."

I grinned. This could be fun. I've never had the opportunity to name anyone before. Would he go for Ralph? I smirked.

"I saw that smirk," he said. "Be nice."

I stared at him and said, "Brett."

A puzzled look cast over his face.

"It's a good name," I said.

"Why Brett?"

"It seems to suit you. It's a strong and handsome name," I said. "But don't let it go to your head."

"You're turning red."

"I know. I always turn red."

Pete came out with a giant platter with cheese fondue and everything that you could possibly want to stick in it . . . and I could think of a lot. I looked at Brett and shook my head. Food first, then fun.

I started salivating. I had nearly forgotten how hungry I was. I picked up the spear and stabbed a cauliflower floret. I then moved to the bread. I was about to head over to the apples when I became aware of Brett's eyes set intently on me. I looked up from my spear to find Brett watching me.

"I'm hungry," I explained. "I haven't eaten for . . . thirty hours." I checked my watch.

"Why not?"

"Does there have to be a reason?" I didn't really want to tell him. "Can't a girl just starve herself without getting questioned?"

He examined me with a serious face but didn't say anything. Good, let him assume what he wants, as long as it's not the embarrassing truth.

He gently tugged my hair. "You drive me absolutely crazy."

That makes us even.

* * *

Angela and Pete waved good-bye as we stepped out to the sidewalk. I was about to say goodnight to Brett when I noticed a black town car sitting at the curb near my car.

"Uh-oh."

"What's wrong?" he asked.

"Uh, I forgot to tell you the reason I called today." I glanced at the town car. Brett followed my gaze.

"Who is that?"

"I don't know. They said you have something they want," I said. "I tried to tell them I didn't know you. They said I'd make a good bargaining chip if you didn't cooperate. Now they're here and we're together. What am I going to tell them now?"

"Damn it! Let's take my car."

"But my car is over there."

"Yeah, next to the people who threatened you."

"How will I get my car?"

"Just get into my car. We'll figure it out later."

When I didn't move, he hauled me over his shoulder. His hand rested on my rear as he stomped over to his car. He plunked me down into his Viper.

"You didn't have to manhandle me, you brute."

"Brute?" A sly smile grew. "I kind of like that. I may have to use that as my next stage name."

I groaned.

His car was black and sleek. Just sitting in it made me sexy by association. The seat curved with my body. I was sure it was made for me.

"Nice car," I said as he pulled out of the parking lot. "Can you really afford this working as a dancer?"

"Not really," he said. "Tell me again what happened?"

"On Sunday, a Neanderthal with a tarantula tattoo grabbed me and brought me over to the town car. The window was only cracked, so I didn't see who was inside. The guy in the car said you have something of his."

"You should have told me this sooner."

"I would have, but you keep flustering me. How am I supposed to remember things when you're always . . . doing what you do?"

"Hmmm," he said as the edges of his lips slightly curved. "I know of a way to remedy the problem."

"See, you're doing it again. I had something else to tell you."

"Yeah, like what?"

"I'm pretty sure some lady has gone bonkers for you. I was having lunch with my mom yesterday. When I got back to my car there was a note on the windshield that said I should stay away from you or I'd regret it. It could have been referring to a different guy, but it just seems odd that both of these occurrences happened on the same day. It has to be about you." I thunked my hand to my head. "I must have a death wish to be in the same car with you!"

"Where's the note?" he asked.

"It's in my car, where I should be."

Brett pulled to the curb next to my house. I blinked. How did we get here so fast and without giving him my address?

"How did you know I live here?"

"It's not important," he said. "Tell me about this other guy the note could be about."

He seemed irritated.

"It's not important," I mimicked him. I was playing with elements out of my control, but I was itching to burn off a little built-up steam. Brett had me wound up like a spring ready to vault.

"I just meant so I could rule him or myself out as a target for the note," he said.

"He's an EMT. His name is Evan West. Kym assumed it could be about him because he uses girls like tissues. I'm not one of them, but we are friends and someone may have the wrong idea." I huffed. I can't believe I'd caved. Brett can keep secrets and I blab them. No wonder he doesn't want to tell me anything.

"Was that the guy parked outside Longhorn's you were talking to?"

I thought back to Saturday morning. "You saw us?"

"I watched you get out of your car and walk up to his truck."

I noticed his hands were clenched on the steering wheel.

"And?" I asked.

"And what?"

"That's it?" A thought hit me. He's jealous. That's why he looked at me with his scary, narrow eyes when I left the club. He had no idea that Evan and I weren't seeing each other. And he obviously detected some flirting going on. This jealousy bit was new to me. Should I tread carefully or make him suffer? I smirked—suffer, of course.

"You're jealous," I needled him.

"Good God, you drive me crazy!" He slammed his head back to the headrest, staring at the ceiling for a moment. Brett then glanced at me. It was dark out, but his eyes were burning a hole through me.

"Yes, I was a little jealous. Happy? I caught the way you looked at each other; your eyes were so animated." He paused before adding, "I knew I wanted to be the one who could make you smile like that. I walked over after you entered the club and asked him about you. He said you were the one he was waiting for." Brett's lips curled into a devious smile. "I should have just punched him. It'd have made me feel a whole lot better."

I sat in silence. I didn't know whether to be shocked by Brett or by what Evan had said. I wasn't aware Evan thought about anyone like that, let alone me. I assumed I was just one more fling to be added to the scoreboard. Of course, Evan could've been blowing smoke for the hell of it. He does like to mess with people's heads when he can, especially if a girl is involved.

"Hmmm, that's interesting," I said.

"I just spilled my guts like a complete moron and that's all you're going to say?"

"I believe so. You seem to have a lot of secrets you don't feel the need to share with me. Until you tell me what's going on here, I'm not saying another word except 'goodnight'!" I opened the door and stepped out.

"Hang on. I'm coming in with you just to make sure there aren't any creeps in your house."

"You're not coming in. I'll never get you to leave with my dignity still intact."

He expelled air to keep him calm. "You don't have a choice. Either you let me look around your house, or I'm taking you home with me and then, believe me, you'll definitely lose all dignity," he said. His eyes pinned me and his lips tightened, waiting for my answer.

Jeez, I liked him better when he was trying to get in my pants. "Fine, search it."

He left me at the door, moving swiftly through the house.

He reappeared with a quizzical look. "What's with the color scheme?"

"You're really going to talk about colors now?"

"No, you're right. I have to go."

Brett stepped past me and out the door. I watched as he angled into his Viper and drove away. No good-bye or a single kiss good-night. I flopped into bed and sulked. Idiot! I scolded myself.

* * *

The next morning I woke up and spotted a crumpled twenty dollar bill on my nightstand. Brett must have left it there last night when he searched my house. With the roller-coaster ride of ups and downs we'd had on our date, it was a sweet touch. As I held the bill, I heated from the image of where it touched him.

If our first date was any indication of what a future would be with him, I should call it quits now. Maybe he won't call me. Then I won't have to worry about it. The thought made me gloomy.

I didn't have time to dwell on it today. I quickly dressed in jeans and a v-neck T-shirt. If I had to do maid of honor duty today, it was going to be wearing comfortable clothes.

My cell phone rang.

"Hey, Mars, it's Jonathan."

"Tell me you have good news for me."

"You're going to love me. I found the cutest heart-shaped lockets. I'll start engraving them today and give you call you when they're finished."

"Jonathan, you always amaze me!" I feigned enthusiasm. I knew he could get the lockets. If there was a dollar to be made on selling gray hair, he'd shave his grandmother bald.

"I do tend to amaze. It'll take me a while to engrave them, so I'll talk to you later," he said and hung up.

I didn't have to arrive at the bridal shop until two, which gave me plenty of time for errands. I made a list in my head. I pondered for a minute until I was jolted by the popping sound of a gun firing rapidly.

I ran to the window to see Mrs. Janowski in the middle of the road firing a gun larger than she was. A dark-blue Suburban raced away and squealed down the street. She shook her fist when the car finally peeled around the corner.

I whipped out of the house and ran across the street.

"Did you see that?" she asked, beaming. "I got 'em on the run!"

"Mrs. J., what are you doing? You can't fire a gun on the street. You nearly gave me a heart attack," I stated. "Where did you get the gun?"

"It's my grandson's paintball gun."

"Oh, thank God. I was afraid you were shooting bullets."

"Wouldn't that be something?" She smiled. "He left it over at my house a few days ago, and I've been itching to use it. It has a sound card and everything. Makes it sound like a machine gun. Good thing, too! Those two no-good scoundrels had it coming. So, I came out here and gave ol' Bessie a test run. They ran with their tails between their legs." She wagged her finger in the direction the car raced off.

I sighed. "Tell me what happened."

"Those two guys were sniffing around your place. They waited outside the whole night and watched your house. At first I called the police, but no one came. I should have known they were going to be useless, so I decided to take care of them myself."

"You should have called the police again. I don't want them hauling you off to jail because you're shooting at suspicious people."

She shouldered her gun. "They'd have to get me first. I'm going to have to get more backup involved with securing the perimeter. This place is going to hell in a hand basket. You want to come in for some coffeecake while I make some phone calls?"

"Thanks, but I have things to do," I said. "Just don't shoot anyone else today."

I watched her scurry back to her house, and I walked back across the street looking for clues or evidence that someone was actually snooping around my house. I didn't know what I was looking for, and I couldn't see anything out of place, except . . . where's my car? A recollection sparked my memory. I had left it at the restaurant.

My cell phone rang.

"Are you okay? I heard a gun being fired."

It was Brett. My pulse kicked up a notch.

"Yes, I'm fine," I answered warily. "And what do you mean you heard a gun being fired? Where are you? Are you the one Mrs. Janowski fired at? And how the hell am I supposed to get my car?" I rapidly fired my round of questions at him.

"Sweet thing, calm down," he sighed. "I can see you're in the same mood as I left you."

"Calm down? Calm down! How can I possibly calm down with people following me, an old lady going bonkers and shooting at people, and no possible mode to escape from this loony bin? I'm stuck here with all the nuts!"

"Are you done?"

I sucked in air. "For now."

"Do you know who she shot at?"

"It was a blue Suburban, and it was only a paintball gun."

He gave an amused chuckle. "Tell her to stop shooting them. I know who they are."

"Of course you would know them. Are you having me followed?"

"Yes, but only for your protection."

"I don't see how they're going to protect me when they run away from a paintball gun. Anyway, tell Mrs. J. yourself. She's all hopped up on adrenaline. If I go over there now, she'll probably shoot me by accident. Are you coming over to drive me to my car?"

"Your dad is on his way to pick you up. I don't feel safe with you right now. You might kick me again," he teased.

"My dad? When did you call my dad?"

"Sweet thing, I have to go," he said, dodging the question. "But if Mrs. J. does shoot you with paintballs, just call me. I'll be more than happy to come over and scrub the paint off."

He hung up. Damn, he irritates the hell out of me. He always seems to be one step ahead and know everything about me. I don't even know his name. He didn't even say when he'd see me again.

I settled on my porch, and within a couple of minutes, my dad pulled into my driveway.

He rolled down the window. "Hop on in. I heard you need a ride to your car."

My dad is a cool, outer-space geek. He's always gazing up at the night's sky and pointing out stars and constellations. One night, when I was really young, he roused me out of bed to go outside where he pointed to a red dot called Mars. I often wondered what would've happened if he'd pulled me out to see a blue dot instead. Would my nickname be Uranus?

Through the years, he's gathered books, charts, telescopes, and other stargazing paraphernalia and keeps them tucked away in a little shed in the backyard. This was where he did his stargazing. He said it was darker in the backyard, away from the house. This may be true, but I believed it was because it was quiet and secluded—away from the noise of everyday life.

"It's over by Pete and Angela's restaurant," I said.

"Who was it that called me? He seemed like a nice man."

"I had a date with him last night. He drove me home, and I left my car at the restaurant," I explained.

"When you bring him over to dinner, I'll take out my telescope and give him the night-sky tour."

"I can't bring anyone to dinner right now. I'm swamped with work. Plus, I have Kym's rehearsal dinner on Friday and her wedding on Saturday."

"But we already arranged it for tomorrow night."

"What do mean it's already arranged?"

"Well, when he called me, he seemed like a nice man. I mean, not many men would call their date's father on her behalf to make arrangements for a ride. So, I asked him what he thought of the universe. He replied it was too big to even comprehend." Dad nodded knowingly. "That shows he knows his place in the world."

I'm not sure how that shows anything, but he seemed to pass my dad's challenge question.

"That doesn't answer my question."

"I asked him if he liked to stargaze, and he said that he never did. Can you imagine that?" He shook his head. "I told him to come over and stargaze with me. He said you both were free on Wednesday night."

"Oh, Dad, the guy could be a nutcase, and you just fixed me up with him again."

"Hmm. Well, when you come over on Wednesday, I'll ask him more questions about the universe. That should settle any doubts," he said reassuringly as he patted my knee.

What just happened?

"Is there something I should know about?" Dad asked.

I looked over at him and followed the direction of his eyes. I gasped when I caught sight of my car. SLUT, WHORE and a few other colorful adjectives were spray-painted all over, covering the car completely.

"Shit!"

"I take it you didn't write this," he said. "And really, Mars, that's not the language a father wants to hear."

"I didn't graffiti my own car!"

"Do you want me to call the police?"

"No, I'll deal with it later."

I stomped over to my car, got in, and slammed the door shut. My dad drove off once I had started my car and pulled away from the curb.

I had to get to the bottom of this fiasco. Somehow I had wedged myself in the middle of scary men with a mission and a psycho stalker. I had no idea if it was the same person or several people. What I did know was that I needed to start taking action on my own. Brett seemed to be a great guy and all, but he's not the one that this is happening to.

Chapter 6

I've never investigated anything in my life, but I did watch enough detective shows to know I should probably start at the beginning with Longhorn's. Annie may be able to tell me more.

I drove the short distance to Longhorn's and parked in the empty lot. There didn't seem to be anyone around. I tried the front door and found it open.

"Hello?" I called.

Annie came out of the small office near the bar. She recognized me and waved me in.

"Hi, Mars. I was just opening up. Come in and have a seat." She motioned to the barstool. "Can I get you anything?"

"No, thank you," I replied. "I came here to talk to you."

"Me? About what?"

"Well, I seem to be stuck in the middle of something, and I don't know what's happening."

"Tell me what it is." She smiled politely. "I'm used to hearing about problems; it comes with the job. I may be able to help."

"I'm hoping you can. It started on Saturday when I came to the club. Two guys saw Brett and me talking, and they assumed I'd be able to convince Brett to give them whatever it is they are looking for."

"Who's Brett?"

"Oh, I'm sorry, it's Nick. He had so many names I made up a new one that I could remember."

Annie laughed. "I can see how that could be confusing. He does like to make up new names all the time."

"Tell me about it. I told Brett these guys are looking for him, but now I'm getting threatening messages from someone else to stay away. I can't figure out if they mean Brett or someone else." I sighed and put my palms up. "I don't know what's going on, but I need to start figuring out some answers."

"Sounds like a lot of trouble," she said. "How do you need me to help?"

"I was hoping you could tell me about the dancer that was murdered."

"Hmm . . . I can't tell you much, because I don't know much about him," she said. "I only started working here a little before Brett."

"Did he seem like a nice guy?"

"No, he wasn't nice. He was very arrogant. I stayed away from him because he always had a dark expression on his face," she said. "It's hard to explain, but I wasn't comfortable around him."

"Do you know if the police found the killer?"

"I don't believe so."

"I don't suppose you have a picture of Jesse?" I asked.

"Yes, I do. The office keeps headshots for promotions."

Annie disappeared into the office and retrieved a headshot and a full-body photo.

He was definitely handsome, but there was something more. His cold eyes peered back at me from the photo and captured my attention. I've seen him someplace before—maybe a month ago. But where?

"I can see what you mean about the dark expression," I said, returning the photos. "I'm sure I've seen him before, but I can't remember where."

"He used to do a lot of promotion for Longhorn's. Perhaps it was at a party."

"That could be," I said then changed my line of questioning. "Do you know of anyone who might stalk Brett?"

"There are two ladies that are regulars here. They come to see Brett, give him all their money, and then leave. But I'm not sure they'd go as far as stalking."

"Do you happen to know their names?"

"Martha, but people call her Marty. I don't know her last name. The other lady I saw you talk to on Saturday. Um," she said with a pause. "Jocelyn, that's her name."

"Jocelyn McCain?" I asked, astonished.

"Yeah, that's the one," Annie said. "Are you okay?"

"I'm just shocked," I said, trying not to grimace. "I'll be fine."

I thanked Annie for her time and left. I was no closer to figuring this out. I couldn't see Jocelyn writing notes or spraying graffiti on my car. Knowing her, she'd fire me. Perhaps it was Marty, but I didn't know who Marty was.

As I drove down the street, pedestrians gawked at my car. Some cars even came to a complete stop as I drove by. I wanted to yell, "I'm really not a slut or whore," but then they'd assume I was a screwball on top of it. This is so embarrassing.

A body shop sign was up ahead. I veered over, pulling into the lot. The men in the garage glanced up from their work as I parked.

I stepped out of the car, threw my shoulders back in an attempt to look purposeful, and strutted to the office. My cheeks flushed. They stared at the graffiti on the car and then stared at me. I hoped they weren't trying to figure out if the graffiti was true.

A man in his early fifties with a small keg for a belly opened the office door and let me inside. He peered behind me and gave a small nod.

"I was going to ask what I could help you with, but I have a feeling I already know."

"Is there anything you can do?"

"Yep," he scratched his belly, "we can paint your car."

"Is that expensive?"

"Is it on all four sides of the car?"

"Yes."

He nodded his head again, shifting his weight to his heels. "Let me crunch some numbers for you, and then we can figure out what we're dealing with."

I gazed out the window as I heard the clickity-clack of his calculator. The men in the garage had gone back to work.

"Okay, this is what I have for you," he said, handing me the estimate.

I inhaled sharply when I read the total and choked. I couldn't pay that.

"Um," I said, shifting my weight, "thank you, but I can't afford this right now."

"We have in-house financing, if you want," he offered. "You'd just have to pay off the balance within one year."

"Let me think about it for a little bit. How long is the estimate good for?"

"'Til the end of the month," he said. "Hang on a second." He dug through his desk and handed me a piece of paper with instructions on it. "Give this a try. You may be able to wash your car and do a few of these steps. It doesn't always work, but if anything, it may smudge the paint so you can't read the graffiti."

I reviewed the list. I'd need dish soap, nail polish remover, and clay. It looked like a long shot, but I was willing to take a chance. Otherwise, I'd repaint, but there was no way I could pay for it. I could possibly take the financing option and try to scrape by. I could also eat mac and cheese for months on end to help save money. I shuddered. Even though I like mac and cheese, the promise of it daily made my stomach turn to lead.

As I opened my car door and slid in, I heard a wolf whistle coming from the garage. My eyes shot over. Everyone was bent down working. They've obviously practiced and perfected their undercover wolf whistle technique.

I stopped at a couple of stores and purchased the listed supplies. Then I drove through a Quik 'n Yummy drive-thru. Their burgers were okay in a pinch, but the place should really be called "Cheap 'n Edible."

I was running out of time, so I dropped the supplies off at home and drove straight to the bridal shop.

Kym, her cousin Fran, and Jim's sister, Kate, were all waiting outside for me. Their eyes widened when I drove my spray-painted car into the lot and parked next to Kym's brand-new red Fiat—an engagement gift from Jim.

"What happened to your car?" Kym asked.

"I left it at Pete and Angela's restaurant overnight and came back to find it spray-painted."

"It's another message from the crazy stalker," Kym gasped.

"I believe so."

"Who were you with?"

"Brett."

"Who's that?"

"Oh, I've given that name to the cowboy. He said he couldn't tell me his name for another week, so I named him."

"God, this gets juicier and juicier," she squealed. "Tell me everything that happened."

"Nothing happened. Let's just go inside."

Kym pinched her lips together. "By the way, you're late!" she scolded. "I swear, I don't know how you can be an events coordinator if you don't even show up on time."

"I'm only a few minutes late, and I've never been late for an event."

We walked in with Kym in the lead. I've been here a few times to help clients. This would be my second fitting for Kym's wedding. I hated fittings. They push, pull, heave, and come at you with pins the size of epidural needles. They tell me not to gain or lose weight, which is impossible. I'm always afraid they will stick me with their monstrous pins if I don't do what they say.

Jim's sister, Kate, changed first and was inspected by Dominique to see if she needed any alterations. Dominique gave Kate an approving nod. Of course. Because she's perfect, just like Jim.

Kym's cousin Fran was second. Dominique turned her around and pulled at her hems.

She nodded. "Yes, this will do nicely."

My turn, I whimpered. I undressed and unhooked the dress from the hanger. I sucked in my stomach to give me extra room and shimmied into the dress.

Since it's an outdoor wedding in summer, Kym wanted to make sure the bridesmaids would be cool and comfortable. This decision prompted her to pick out short, sheer dresses that were most likely designed for the cover of a lingerie catalog. We'd be cool all right, but we'd also be highly exposed. We were going to look like Bride Goldilocks and the Three Tramps. Please, let me remember not to bend over at the wedding.

Dominique helped with the zipper. "You gained weight!"

"But the zipper is all the way up. Where did I gain weight?"

Kym's eyes rounded. "Your boobs!"

I turned to the mirror. My boobs bulged out of the top like giant Nerf balls.

"How could I have gained weight? I have no money for food," I stated. "Was the dress altered properly?"

Dominique bristled. "We don't make mistakes."

Kym sent a horrified look to Dominique. "Can you fix it?"

"I don't know. This is going to take a miracle." Dominique inspected the seams. "I can let it out a little bit more. I may be able to add a little fabric to the sides without it being noticeable." She turned to me. "Try to lose a little weight, just in case."

"It might be easier if you found a smaller-chested woman to be your maid of honor," I told Kym.

"Don't you dare try to back out. You'll be in the wedding even if your boobs are hanging out."

Nice visual! I'm stuck with this horrible, orchid-nightie nightmare.

My cell phone rang. I dug through my purse, and then gave up ever finding it in time. I turned my purse upside down and shook it empty before my phone finally fell out, buzzing its way across the purse wreckage.

"Do you have a date for Kym's wedding?" It was Brett.

"I'm not taking anyone since I'm working it and participating in it."

"Not anymore. I'm taking you and the dress you're almost wearing."

How could he know what I'm wearing? I padded over to the window and peeked through it. I couldn't see anyone.

"Sweet thing, if you move around much more, you'll have the neighborhood gathering at the window, and I'll have to come in and rescue you," he said huskily. "But I don't rescue anyone for free."

"Where are you?"

"It's not important. I'll talk to you later," he said and hung up.

I looked down at the phone. I didn't even get to yell at him for weaseling dinner out of my dad tomorrow night.

"Kym, do you still have me down for a guest at your wedding?"

"Yes. If you don't take someone, I'll pull a random man off the street. You better pray it's not a homeless man."

I sighed. I had no doubt she'd arrange for a homeless man to be my date.

* * *

I was heading back to the parking lot when Kym called out, "Remember, we're meeting at my house tonight. Make sure to bring everything with you."

The wedding favors! I had forgotten to pick up the supplies.

"Sure, no problem," I said a little too happily.

Kym glared but she didn't say anything.

I ran to my car and jumped in. This was going to be the longest day ever.

I stopped by the liquor store to pick up several cases of mini champagne bottles. I then proceeded to speed to the printer to pick up the labels and programs. My last stop was the fabric store for yards of ribbon.

"What kind of ribbon do you need?" the sales woman asked.

"I need ribbon for wedding favors."

"What's the color scheme?"

"I think it's pink."

"You think?" she asked, peering over her spectacles.

"I'm not sure." I racked my brain.

She sighed. "Perhaps you should find out before we go to the trouble of cutting ribbon you can't return."

"I need to buy ribbon—and soon—or the bride will kill me," I said. "How about white?"

"Do you know what shade of white?"

Ugh! I should know that. What happened to all my training as an events coordinator?

"Let me call my coworker and find out."

The sales woman frowned and turned to help a woman who had just entered the store. I quickly dialed the office number.

"Emmy, what colors are we using in Kym's wedding?"

"Don't you already know?"

"Emmy," I whined. "Please, just give me the colors. My world has gone topsy-turvy. I can't remember anything anymore."

"Hang on."

She came back on the phone a couple of minutes later. "Are you still there?" she asked.

"Yes. What are the colors?"

"Maybe you should go see a doctor; it's not like you to forget. You may be coming down with a case of dementia."

"Emmy! I'm only thirty years old."

"It's been known to happen in freak cases. You should get checked out."

"I don't have dementia. I have a crappy-ass life, and it's currently getting the better of me."

The sales woman's eyes slid over to me, giving me a stare down only a librarian could appreciate.

"I was just trying to be helpful. The color scheme is orchid and the linens are snowy white."

I smacked my hand against my forehead. Of course the color was orchid. I have a bridesmaid dress that color. How could I not remember? Maybe Emmy's right. I could have early dementia. That may explain how my keys mysteriously end up in unexpected places. Last week, I found them in the freezer. I'm sure the chocolate-chip cookie dough ice cream had nothing to do with it.

I bought a spool of orchid-colored ribbon and a snowy-white spool, too. A girl needs to cover all her bases when heading into a battlefield. Don't let the term "wedding" fool you; it's not all doves and cake.

I fanned out my shirt to keep it from sticking to me. I was in a complete head-to-toe sweat and had just a half-hour before I was due at Kym's. It was just enough time to go home and shower.

* * *

Mrs. Janowski was on her porch when I pulled into my driveway. She shuffled over in her powder-blue polyester pants and matching floral-print shirt. She carried a wooden bat at her side.

"Mars, I just had to come over," she said anxiously. "There was a big scary man with a tarantula tattoo on his neck. He was pounding on your door and looking in your windows. He waited for you for about thirty minutes and then left."

"Was there a man in the back seat of the town car?"

"There was a town car, but I couldn't see. But now that you mention it, I did notice the back window was cracked down a couple of inches."

Mrs. Janowski handed me the wooden bat. "Here, I want you to keep this with you," she said. "Make sure to take it to bed with you, too."

I thanked Mrs. J. for the bat and hurried inside. I bolted the door behind me. Thank God I hadn't been home when they were here.

I took the bat into the shower with me.

Twenty minutes later, I was refreshed and jogged out the door. I had five minutes to get to Kym's without her yelling at me. Needless to say, I hauled ass.

* * *

Kym had a selection of wine opened and ready. Decadent truffles and small cakes sat prettily on decorative plates. Fran and Kate sat talking on the couch. Kym handed me a wine glass filled with velvety red liquid that played softly on my tongue.

"This must be from Jim's wine collection," I said.

Kym nodded. "He brought it over this afternoon."

I eyed the sweets.

"Don't you dare," she scolded.

"But they look so good."

"You need to lose weight so you can fit into your dress."

"This is so unfair. How am I supposed to lose weight in my boobs?" I asked. "It's not like I can do boob crunches."

"You could try. What I do know is you're not going to eat sweets," she said, handing me a bowl of cut carrots and celery. "You can eat this instead."

I looked at the bowl and winced. Lunch was long gone from my stomach, and I was supposed to eat a bowl of rabbit food. This isn't a wedding; it's torture.

The girls helped carry in the supplies from my car, arranging them in assembly-line fashion.

I pulled out the champagne bottles and stuck a personalized label on it. Kym tied a ribbon with a silver heart to the neck and put it back in the box. Fran and Kate were in charge of making fans out of the wedding programs.

I sipped my wine and left the veggies in the corner where they belonged. I refilled my fourth glass when Kym asked, "Did you ever call Evan to see if he knows anyone who might try to take revenge on you?"

"No, I can't call him. He's too tasty. I bet one night with Evan would feel like heaven . . . Heaven Evan." I giggled and slapped a hand over my mouth. Without food in my stomach, the wine was going straight to my head.

Fran and Kate peeked over at me with raised eyebrows.

"I'm going to call him for you," Kym said.

"No, you can't. I'll feel stupid."

"You already look stupid driving around with a spray-painted car."

"True, but he's so cute, and he scares me a little."

"You're only afraid of him because he talks to you the way you dream a man would." She poked my arm, sliding me a smile.

Kym stole my phone and found him in the contacts. I quickly refilled my wine glass and downed it.

"Evan?" She asked and paused to listen. "Uh, thank you for the naughty invitation." Kym winked at me. "But, no, you'll have to ask Mars when you talk to her. This is Kym. I'm a friend of Mars."

He's probably hitting on her right now. He's really good at that. He transcended the need for words. One look into his translucent blue eyes and I break out into a sweat.

"She's been threatened by a woman who's telling her to back off and leave some guy alone. We can't figure out who the guy is. I thought you might have a stalker since you have such a reputation," she teased.

Kym nodded. "Yeah, she's here. She's had too much to drink though." She eyed me. "Okay, you can talk to her. If she doesn't make sense, please ignore her." She handed me the phone.

"Heaven Evan?" Somewhere in my brain, a voice drifted down to tell me to shut up.

"Mars, are you okay?" Evan asked. "Do you need me to come and take you home? I could tuck you into bed and make you feel better?"

"Your eyes are blue like glacier ice. Can I lick them?"

The room tilted and grew fuzzy. I waved my hand in front of my face. I couldn't see it. "Heaven Evan, I think I'm already in bed. Someone turned out the lights. I need a nightlight. Oh, your eyes could be my nightlight."

Chapter 7

I awoke to a dark room. I dragged myself up from Kym's couch, untangling my legs from the pile of blankets tucked around me. My mouth tasted fuzzy and dry. I wiped my hand against my lips and felt crusted drool on the corner of my mouth. Beautiful!

I stood but had to sit again until the room stopped spinning. I glanced at the clock on the wall. It read a little after one. What happened? Wine. I remember wine. I couldn't recall anything beyond that.

I was ready to crawl back under the blankets and die, but heaven had to wait until I brushed my teeth. I licked the front of my teeth. Ick! Even heaven wouldn't want me with these teeth. Heaven? Something in my mind sparked, but I didn't know what or why.

I trudged to the car and slowly drove home. Fifteen minutes later, I was up in my bathroom scouring off the last of the murky wine aftertaste.

I peeled off my clothes and pulled out the first T-shirt nearest to me, which was small and short. I didn't care that it didn't cover my undies; I just wanted my pillow.

I remembered Mrs. Janowski's bat downstairs. I drug myself downstairs and retrieved it. I may be tired, but not tired enough to forget the demented people who were bound and determined to find me.

I drifted to sleep, cuddling with my bat. I found myself sitting on a glacier. Why am I on a glacier? I heard noises coming from behind the gigantic ice rock. Someone was opening the door. Wait, there's no door on a glacier. My eyes popped open.

I held my breath, straining to hear. It was quiet. I let out a calming breath but caught it as I heard the bedroom door handle turn. I snatched the bat from the bed. My legs wouldn't move. I sat frozen on the bed. The door opened and a shadow moved in, closing the door behind it. Shit! My adrenaline kicked in and I quickly stood.

I could sense the person was near me. My stomach dropped. I closed my eyes and swung the bat. A vibration zapped through my arm as the bat connected. Thud! A body crumpled to the floor.

"Damn it!" a deep voice growled.

I hopped over the shadowy mass and flicked on the lights. Brett was sprawled on the floor, clutching his side.

"What the hell are you doing here? I could have killed you!" I scolded.

"You hit me with a bat, not a grenade," he stated with an edge of pain.

"Can you get up?" I asked.

"I'll need help. You may have broken a rib."

"See? I could've killed you."

"Just help me up, killer."

I helped him to his knees and then pulled him onto the bed.

"Why didn't you ring the doorbell like a normal person?"

He smiled through gritted teeth. "I couldn't fall asleep. I tossed and turned, remembering you in that little dress from earlier. I figured if you could haunt my dreams, then I may as well come here and we could be sleepless together." He grazed my leg with his finger.

My skin erupted with tingles. "How did you get in here?"

"Seriously?" he asked.

"Yes."

"You have a fake rock outside your door with a key in it. Any idiot could open the door."

"You noticed it?"

"Sweet thing, the rock's paint is peeling."

"Oh," I said.

I made a mental note to buy a better fake rock.

His eyes focused on me. He was sitting on the bed a couple of feet away from me. His expression darkened as his eyes traveled from my small T-shirt down to my panties.

"This may be better than the dress." His arm reached around my legs, pulling me in to straddle him. His hands roamed from my legs up to my hips. His touch singed my skin. Hot tingles awoke my long-suppressed appetite.

His lips pressed against my exposed stomach. He settled me firmly on his lap. Brett held eye contact with me as his hand found its way under my shirt. His hand explored, stopping to cup my breast. His thumb gently played and circled my nipple. A moan escaped my lips, and he gave me a slow, easy grin, giving me a glimpse of his white, predatory teeth.

He drew my mouth to his. His tongue raced across my bottom lip, and I parted to let him in. My arms and legs wrapped around him. I gasped as I settled, feeling his hard manhood beneath me.

He's . . . perfect.

Brett turned so he could position us better on the bed.

"Damn!" he barked.

I jumped off.

He clenched his side. "Sweet thing, you need to take me to the hospital."

I left him on the bed while I threw on jeans and shoes.

"I'm going to have to lean on you," he gritted. His breath hitched, and he winced. "I'm having a hard time breathing."

With my help, he dragged himself up to stand. As we clomped down the stairs, I concentrated on not falling as the weight of him beared down on my shoulders.

I helped him into the passenger seat of his car. His face was white and lined with pain.

I killed him! If he recovers, he'll kill me. I stopped to think. Kill me with strangulation or maybe with steamy revenge sex. I wasn't sure which, but I was really hoping for the second option.

I drove to the emergency room, glancing over to see if he was okay. His eyes were closed and his jaw was clenched. I pulled in front of the emergency wing and dashed over to the wheelchairs.

"You're not putting me in a wheelchair," he said between gritted teeth.

"You're going to sit in the wheelchair whether you like it or not," I replied.

"I've never sat in a wheelchair, and I'm not going to now."

Was this some man thing? Can't be seen with a slight weakness even though he's in visible pain?

"I can't hold your weight. If you don't sit in the wheelchair I'm going to punch you in the ribs and push you into the wheelchair."

His eyes opened wide, shocked that I'd threaten something like that. A slow smile curled on his lips. "I have the feeling you could give me a run for my money," he said, dragging himself out of the car to sit in the wheelchair.

I parked him in the waiting room while I made my way to the front desk.

The woman at the desk barely glanced up when I stepped in front of her. "Yes?" she asked.

"My friend was hit in the ribs with a bat. He said one may be broken."

She glanced around me to view Brett. "That's him?"

"Yes," I replied.

"Okay, I'll get someone to take him back. In the meantime, fill out these papers and give them back to me." She handed me a clipboard with an inch of forms.

I settled into a chair next to Brett. "They want you to fill out these papers."

He scowled at the papers. "I can't move my arm."

"Well, I can't fill them out. I don't even know your name."

He shot me glance. "Reach into my pocket and grab my wallet. I have my insurance card in there."

I reached carefully into the front pocket of his jeans, trying not to touch anything I'd be sorry for later. I retrieved a black leather wallet. I grinned like a child who was given a whole box of cookies.

Brett glowered at me. "Don't look so happy."

I ignored him and opened the wallet, deliberately taking my time and savoring the mystery that was about to unravel.

It had marks on the inside from something that used to belong there. I traced the outline with my thumb. If my super sleuth-like senses—and the cop shows I've seen—were correct, a badge used to live in this spot. My senses didn't tell me what kind of badge. He must have worked for some part of the government until recently. I slid my eyes to over him, but his were cold. I smiled sweetly, knowing this must be driving him crazy. And to drive him a little more over the edge, I pulled out his driver's license. I'll harass him about the missing badge later.

The license was issued in Texas under the name of Brett Thompson. My mouth dropped open.

"Careful," he warned, "I can find a use for that mouth of yours."

"Your name is Brett?"

"Yes, now fill out the form so I can get some help."

"Why didn't you just tell me at the restaurant when I guessed it?"

"Sweet thing, if you knew my name, you'd be one more step in this mess."

I didn't see how knowing his name would involve me any more than I already was.

"You need to tell me what's going on."

"I will. But not tonight."

He must be on the verge of passing out from pain, but I still wanted to know more information—now!

"Why don't you have a Texan accent?"

"I didn't move there until I was fifteen. I have a slight accent that disappears when I'm farther north."

I filled in the forms and asked Brett about his family medical history. He spouted short, clip answers. I itched to ask one more question that wasn't on the questionnaire.

"Have you ever been shot?"

"Yes."

I tried to sound like I was reading the questions from the form. "How many times? And in what part of the body?"

"Look at me," he said.

I turned to face him. My mouth twitched.

"You're horrible at lying. I've been shot twice; once in my shoulder, and once in the leg."

"Hmmm, you must not be very good at your job if you keep getting shot," I said.

A vein in his neck pulsed and I chuckled.

I stood and handed the forms to the woman at the desk. A few minutes later a nurse arrived to fetch Brett.

"Do you want me to go in with you?" I asked.

"No, I'm afraid I'm going to cry. Then I'll never hear the end of it."

The nurse wheeled him through double doors and out of sight. I leaned my head back against the seat, getting as comfortable as one possibly could in a hard plastic chair, and closed my eyes. I wasn't sure how long I'd be sitting here, so I might be able to get a few minutes of sleep. I dreaded working on no sleep.

A warm breath fell lightly across my ear and a sweet, slow kiss traveled down the side of my neck to my shoulder. How is Brett out of the ER so fast? I opened my eyes to find Evan.

"You taste like vanilla," he whispered in my ear.

I blinked at the sight of him. "What are you doing here?"

"I just brought in a man who had a panic attack," he said. Evan searched my eyes as if giving me an exam. "I should be asking you what you're doing here. The last time I talked to you, you passed out from too much wine."

"Did I talk to you?" I attempted to rewind to earlier this evening. "I can't remember anything. Kym wouldn't let me eat because I couldn't fit into a certain, um, area of my bridesmaid dress. I woke up on Kym's couch, drove home, and went to bed."

Evan studied my small T-shirt for a moment. "Then why are you here?"

"Well, I remember I was dreaming about a glacier." I stopped when a playful smile flickered on Evan's face. "What?"

"Nothing. Go on."

"The door on the glacier opened. I figured something wasn't right. I woke to find someone entering my house, and I hit him with a bat. I brought him here because he may have a broken rib."

Worried etched Evan's face. "Are you okay? Did you call the police?"

"I'm fine," I reassured. "It was just Brett. I probably would've hit him anyway for breaking in, but I wouldn't have hit him so hard. Just hard enough to give him a good bruise."

"Who's Brett?"

"I think you met him on Saturday morning. He was at the club."

Evan thought for a moment and nodded. "He asked me about you."

"I heard."

A silent pause ballooned between us.

"He took the key from the rock, didn't he?"

"You know about the rock?"

"Sugar, it's a very sad, peeling rock. It's kind of hard to miss that it's a fake."

I gazed into Evan's eyes and became lost in flecks of blue. Content to just stare, I couldn't stay focused on what he was saying.

He pulled me to my feet. "Walk me out to my truck."

"I'm tired."

"It won't take long." Evan slung his arm around my shoulder and kissed my temple. We strolled to his UrgentMed truck.

"You know you could have called me. I would have brought the guy down here," he said. "You can call me anytime for anything."

My knees softened at the image that passed through my mind.

"I couldn't call you. You'd be no better than Brett," I said.

He smiled and gently pinned me against the truck. His leg slid between mine as he leaned into me.

My hormones were already on turbo charge from Brett. With Evan on the prowl, I was about ready to come unhinged.

I searched for an escape until Evan tilted his head down. His hair fell across his face, framing his eyes. My heart hitched as his mouth moved toward mine. He seized my waiting lips with his.

I had waited too long for this moment. I flung my arms around his neck, drawing him in to deepen the kiss. Evan was momentarily surprised but recovered quickly, impatient for more. He lifted me. His weight pressing me harder into the truck, I wrapped my legs around his waist. My thighs burned from the contact. He grasped my hair, gently tugging it back. As my head followed, he gained access to my neck and shoulders.

I was breathless for a moment until I exhaled, "Oh, God."

A call came through on the radio. It was dispatch giving out orders for Evan.

"Dear Lord, Mars," he growled in my ear, then he nuzzled into my neck. "I should have kissed you years ago."

"I wouldn't have let you," I said, sounding calmer than I felt.

His eyes brightened deviously, "You mean you'll let me now?"

"Kind of obvious, isn't it? But don't you have go?"

"No, I quit." He kissed the nape of my neck. The tip of his tongue barely grazed my skin, sending a ripple of awareness through me. "My new job is to make you so unbelievably happy your head will spin."

"Put me down and go," I insisted, unwrapping myself from him. I had to get distance between us.

Evan set me down. "Don't forget where we left off." He slid into the truck.

I watched him drive until he was out of view. He left me wanting more. My thighs hummed with desire. This was what it must have felt like for the countless women who were ravaged by him and then left at the curb wanting more.

I could kick myself. I had contact with two incredibly hunky men and I turn into a heap of hormones. Where's my self-control? One word or look and I can't keep my hands off.

I should keep the graffiti on my car as punishment.

As I returned to the waiting room, Brett was wheeled out and he was really happy. A twinge of guilt fluttered through my stomach. I tried to shake it off, but it hunkered down. We'd only had one date, and I just found out his name tonight. We're hardly attached, I reminded myself.

The nurse wheeled him over and handed me a white paper bag filled with medications. "Are you his wife?" she asked.

"Just a friend."

"Oh, okay." She seemed puzzled. "Well, we gave him some strong pain medication and it's been making him a little loopy. He said something about his wife being on Mars or something like that.

"He has a cracked rib, so he'll have to relax and not do anything strenuous. The doctor put a few notes and recommendations in the bag for you. We told Brett, but with the drugs in his system, he probably won't remember. Make sure he stays with someone tonight in case there are any adverse reactions to the medications. And watch yourself," she warned. "He's been a bit fresh with his hands." And on cue, he slapped her ass.

"Oh!" she yelped. "If you weren't a patient . . . and cute, I'd slap you." She rubbed her backside as she hurried away.

The guilt dissolved instantly. Idiot.

I drove him to my house since the address on his driver's license still listed him with a Texas address and he was uncooperative in telling me where he was staying.

We reached the front door. I brought the key to the lock, but the door was cracked open. I pushed it open the rest of the way and peered in. Brett was in no shape to help as a bodyguard, so I left him on the porch. I cautiously stepped in and turned on the light.

I gasped at the destruction that littered the living room and kitchen. Drawers were torn out and emptied, tables were tipped over, and couch cushions and pillows were slashed open. Spray-painted on the wall in slanted handwriting was a message:

Your time is running out. The Hammer will come down on you next.

I studied the gaping holes in the wall near the message. It looked like it was beaten in by a sledgehammer. Great, death by sledgehammer. Lucky me!

Weary with fatigue, I couldn't even muster enough energy to be terrified. Brett didn't seem to be bothered at all. I turned around to find him passed out on the couch, resting his head on the cushion stuffing.

I heaved myself upstairs to crawl into bed—or what was left of it. Someone had taken a knife to it. The stuffing bulged out, exposing the springs. I threw the comforter over it then threw myself on top.

Chapter 8

I was sleeping when I heard footsteps fall near me and felt a warm kiss press onto my temple. I tried to wake up, but my eyelids wouldn't budge.

"I'll see you later, sweet thing," a voice said.

I fell back into a deep sleep.

It was eleven o'clock when I finally woke up. I stared around the room in disbelief. Now that the sun lit the room, I could see how much damage there was. Everything was dumped, tipped over, and searched. I tiptoed through the house. It was the same in every room. The living room was the only room that had a message spray-painted on the wall and sledgehammer damage.

My skin crawled with unease.

This didn't make any sense. Why would the Hammer nut-job go to the trouble of ransacking the house?

I started to pick up the mess when my cell phone rang.

"Hi, Kym."

"How are you feeling?"

"Oh, just dandy," I said.

The rooms were overwhelmingly annihilated, I thought to myself. How did I manage to collect so much stuff?

"You saying it and meaning it are two different things."

"I've just had a very long and horrible evening." Except for the kissing, I reminded myself.

"Oh, no! You'll have to tell me everything, but I have to tell you something first." She hesitated. "You may want to sit down."

"There's nothing you could say that will bother me at this point." Plus, there wasn't anything to sit on.

"Last night, before you passed out, I called Evan to ask if he would know of anyone crazy enough to stalk him or harass you. Do you remember?"

"I don't remember anything except for something about glaciers."

"Do you remember what you said to Evan about glaciers?"

"No, but I bumped into him last night in the ER. I told him about having a weird dream about glaciers. He seemed amused, but I don't know why."

"Uh oh."

"What?" I panicked. "What did I do?"

"Before you passed out, you told him he had blue eyes like glacier ice."

"Well, that's not too bad." I relaxed. "He does have beautiful eyes."

"I know he has beautiful eyes, but you also asked him if you could lick them. You also called him Heaven Evan."

"I did not!"

"You did, and then you passed out. I warned him you were saying weird things before I let him talk to you, but I wanted to warn you in case you saw him. I guess I'm too late."

I groaned. There's the icing on top of the dog-poop cake.

I shared the details of everything that had happened since I left her place, editing out a few juicy tidbits along the way. We hung up after she extracted every single juicy detail from me. I never could keep anything from her.

When I hung up, I saw I had ten missed calls from work.

I ran back upstairs to dress. The Stevenson party was Friday, and I had Mayor Fenwig's luncheon tomorrow. All of the details had been worked out for the luncheon long ago, but there are always last-minute changes or complications that pop up when you least expect them.

I dressed in a flurry and ran back downstairs. As I looked around the living room, a weight pressed down on me. I'll deal with the cleanup later.

I picked up my keys. Something's wrong. I inspected my keys, realizing that my car key was replaced with a different one. I opened the front door and spied the Viper sitting in the driveway. My car was nowhere to be seen. I hit the unlock button and the Viper flashed his lights at me.

Hello to you, too.

Mrs. Janowski stepped out of her house. "That's a crackerjack of a ride," she called.

"It's not mine. Just on loan," I said, crossing the street.

"Is it from that muscular man who came out of your house this morning?"

I flushed. "Yes," I admitted. "But there's nothing going on. He had to stay the night because I hit him with the bat you gave me."

"Did you?" she asked. "Isn't that something? He did look like he was in pain. I was hoping it was because you gave him a good tumble in the sheets. It's a pity nothing happened between you two. He's a handsome rascal, and you've been too long without a good roll in the hay."

"Mrs. J.!" I turned cherry red. "I'm just fine in that department."

"If you say so," she said, unconvinced. "The last man you entertained was over six months ago, and he was stuffy. I don't see how you could've had any fun with him. Now, the guy you hit with the bat, he looks like he'd know how to curl a woman's toes back."

I can't believe I'm having a sex conversation with Mrs. Janowski.

"I have to get to work," I said. "If you see the blue Suburban, don't shoot. Brett said they're helping him. But if you see any insane women at my house, feel free to shoot them with paintballs, and then call the cops."

"Oh, how exciting," she tittered. "I'll go get ol' Bessie ready."

I returned to my driveway, grinning at the Viper. I slid behind the steering wheel. I could sense Brett in here. His scent lingered, and I felt I was intruding on personal space . . . personal, sexy, hot Brett space. Just sitting in his seat was intoxicating. I turned the key, revving the car engine. A note from Brett perched on the dashboard.

Mars, I took your car to get it painted. Use my car as much as you need. Don't worry about the mess in your house. I'll take care of it today. Pick you up at six for dinner. – Brett. P.S. Feel free to wear the little T-shirt and panties again tonight.

A smile escaped. Damn him. I opened the glove box, about to throw the note in, when I glimpsed a one hundred dollar bill resting on the car manual. That's a little too trusting of him. I closed the glove box with the money left in its place.

* * *

I pulled into the office lot, taking a couple of deep, calming breaths before entering the front door.

"Hi," Emmy said. "I was wondering when I'd see you. You have a few messages on your desk."

"Thanks, Emmy. Anything new?"

"Curtis is having a mental breakdown about the Stevenson dinner, and Jocelyn just got another round of Botox. This time it's in her lips. It looks like she got stung by a dozen bees."

"Her lips were still puffy from the last round," I said.

"I know. One of these days her head is going to explode."

I smiled. "You know how to brighten a girl's day. I'll go check on Curtis."

Curtis is an excellent events coordinator, but he's a bit dramatic when things go bad. Unfortunately, they do go bad. It only takes one drunk, one unskilled chef, one forgetful employee, or one clumsy accident and an event can unravel faster than my freshman home economics sweater.

"Hey, Curtis," I said.

"Oh, Mars! Thank God you're here. I've been going out of my mind," he said. "I'm trying to get a room booked for the party and nothing is available."

"Where have you tried?"

"Everywhere," he said with a flip of his hand.

"Is there anywhere outside we can have it?"

"All the patios and gardens have been booked, too."

"Okay, give me the form they filled out and keep working on the rest of the details. I'll find a location."

Relief washed over his face.

"Oh, and get an estimate on large event tents just in case," I said.

Great! The party is two days away and we have no place to hold it. I should have devoted more time to this. Jocelyn is going to have my head.

I walked to my desk while reading the request form the Stevensons had filled out. With a thoroughly completed request form, the client is able to tell us what the event is for, dates and times, how many people, food they like, colors they prefer, any known allergies, special requests, and my personal favorite is about memories they'd like to include or evoke.

It may be as simple as putting together a slide show with pictures of little Timmy growing up to become a man graduating from college. Each client can tell us specifically what they want, or they can just give us details on a special memory and we can take it and run with it. The Stevensons' memory sparked an idea.

"Curtis, I'll also need quotes for tables, chairs, and outside lighting," I said. "And see if you can find any pretty candle lanterns."

"I've seen that look before," Curtis said. "You have a fabulous idea, don't you?"

"I'll need to go down to the site first."

"You have to take me with you."

"I need you to start working on the quotes."

Curtis gave me a sideward glance. "Honey, I can get these done faster than you can get into those little jeans you're wearing."

"That's not too fast; it takes me forever to get them on."

"I know what you mean. I have a pair just like that."

"You're on your own if Jocelyn has a fit."

We walked outside and headed to the Viper.

"Oooh, girl, look at this car," he gushed.

"It's a loner."

His eyes bounced from me to the car.

"What?" I asked.

"Who's the man?"

"What do you mean?"

"Oh no, you didn't just play dumb!"

"Fine, just get in the car. I'll tell you on the way," I said.

He scrambled into the car. "Look at this car," he said, posing in the Viper. "My testosterone just spiked."

My eyebrow raised.

"Just cause I don't use it doesn't mean I don't have it," he said, smoothing back his wavy brown hair. "Now spill it. I want to hear everything."

"The owner of the car is a guy I met at Kym's bachelorette party."

"From Longhorn's?" he asked.

I nodded.

"But the only guys that'd be at Longhorn's are the . . ." He paused as his eyes widened. He opened his mouth, but nothing came out.

"Dancers." I finished his sentence.

"You got freaky with a dancer?" he asked.

"I didn't get freaky with anyone."

"Mm-hmm."

"I didn't."

"Then how do you explain sitting in an exotic dancer's Viper?" he asked. "Men don't let anyone drive their cars—unless you've given him an overhaul."

"We went out on a date. I cracked his rib with a bat, and the psycho people who are stalking him tore up my house and spray-painted my car."

Curtis narrowed his eyes, pursing his lips. "If you didn't want to tell me, you could've just said so instead of making up a crazy-ass story like that."

I sighed.

I exited the freeway and took a country road down about two miles.

"Here it is," I said, pulling into a small gravel parking area off to the side.

"Mars?" Curtis asked, his voice quiet.

"Yeah?"

"You did it again," Curtis said. "You turned shit into gold."

I smiled. This is the part of the job I loved. Making an event work, despite the curve balls thrown.

We took a few notes on-site then returned to the office. I added more tasks to the growing list of things to do.

"Will you be able to handle this?" I asked, pulling into the office parking lot.

"Now that we have a location, I'm on fire!" he said, jumping out of the car.

I followed him into the office where he flung himself into his chair, kicked his feet up, and picked up the phone.

Yeah, he'll be fine.

I spied the messages stacked neatly on my desk. Most of them I could respond via email. I like to do most of my communications by email. It keeps everything in black and white. Not as many mistakes happen when you have proof of your conversation. I whittled my way down to the last message. It only had a phone number, no name or reason for calling.

"Emmy, do you know who this is from?"

"He wouldn't give me his name," she said. "He said you'd know what it's about."

"I'll take it with me. I have errands to run, but call if you need me."

I stuffed the laptop in my bag and swung out the door. My first stop on the list was Flower Power. Hopefully they hadn't started on the Stevenson order yet.

"Mars!" Gloria exclaimed. "What a surprise! We never get to see you so soon between orders."

"I came to see if you've started the Stevenson order. I was hoping I could change it."

"You came just in time. Willow was going to head to the wholesale market for the order. What did you have in mind?"

I told her about the location and the memory that was filled out on the form.

"Oh, that's inspiring." Gloria clapped her hands together. "I know just what to do."

"Thank you." I gave Gloria a hug. "I can always count on you."

I left the shop, elated the event was taking a turn in the right direction. I called Curtis to tell him the flowers were taken care of. By the time I called, he had already secured the location and had the tents ordered.

It was a little past lunch. I was ravenous from missing breakfast and not eating dinner the night before. Thank you, Kym. I pulled up outside a little café that offered sandwiches and Wi-Fi. I slung the laptop bag over my shoulder.

The café had a shabby-chic vibe to it. It was comfortable and laidback with mismatched furniture and dishes. I ordered the biggest sandwich they had and an iced tea.

I scoped the room, looking for the perfect spot. An oversized squishy chair near the corner window with a small table off to the side called my name. I made my way over there, squeezing past a group of college kids who must have been in summer session by the way their books were strewn across their table and they were hunkered down over them.

I set the iced tea and sandwich on the table and the laptop on my lap. I thumbed through the messages and emailed everyone except for the one with the phone number. I dialed the number and waited.

"Hello, Ms. Cannon," a man's voice answered.

"Hi," I responded. "I have a message you called. But, I'm sorry, I don't know your name."

"No, and you won't."

"May I help you with something?" I asked.

"You can tell lover boy that we mean business. We've already searched your house, and we couldn't find it. I want it now!"

I clenched the phone, turning my knuckles white. "You destroyed my house! I don't know what you want. If you tell me, then I can find it for you."

"Your boyfriend knows what I'm looking for. Give him this phone number and tell him he can arrange an exchange. I'm running out of options. You won't like it when I get to my next option," he threatened.

I ground my teeth. "Did you write the message on my living room wall?"

He gave a tight laugh, "No. But you better watch yourself. We'll make damn sure we get to you first," he said and hung up.

If they didn't leave the message on the wall, then there are definitely two whack-a-doo parties involved. I had really hoped I was just dealing with one nut.

I double-clicked on the Internet icon and typed "Sledgehammer killer" into the search engine. Articles from Texas, Florida, Colorado, and Illinois popped up. The oldest was from Texas, so I started with that one.

Sledgehammer Killer Strikes Houston. Eve Thompson was brutally murdered last night in her home by a person the police are now referring to as the "Sledgehammer Killer."

I stopped reading. Thompson? I'm sure there are hundreds of Thompsons in Houston. But as I turned it over in my head, it was too much of a coincidence not to be true. Brett had to be related to Eve. Why else would someone give up his badge and move to Wisconsin to be an exotic dancer? He knows something; he must be involved. And by him being involved, I've been dragged into it. The stuffy guy Mrs. Janowski referred to is starting to look like a dream catch.

I read about Eve's death and the deaths of five other women. It all happened the same way: They met a male dancer, the stalker threatened the girls to back off; the girls didn't and died by several blows from a sledgehammer.

I had met a male dancer. The stalker has definitely made threats . . . I really don't want to die! I bit back a tear. I was not going to come unglued!

I continued to read every article, every blog, and every site that gave information about the Sledgehammer Killer. Some of the information was false. I refuse to believe the killer is an alien from the planet Hammercon. My head swam with information. The only problem was what to do with the information. How in the world can I catch a serial killer? For God's sake, I dress tables for a living, not hunt down murderers.

Stress was causing a painful kink to tighten in my neck. I only know how to do one thing when I'm stressed, but I'm not allowed to eat cheesecake until after the wedding. The next best thing . . . a spa pedicure.

I called Candi to see if she could squeeze me in. The gods smiled on me; there was a cancellation. I packed up my laptop, sipped the last of the iced tea, and hurried to the car.

* * *

I relaxed contently in the chair. My fingers mindlessly played with the chair massage controls. My feet graciously soaked in hot, bubbling water.

Candi was finishing up with another client while I waited and relaxed. I didn't mind. My thoughts drifted to Brett. Eve must be Brett's sister. The age difference was close enough to make it a possibility. I could see him giving up his life back in Texas to find a serial killer who killed his sister. My breath caught. What if she was his wife? No, that would mean his wife was cheating on him. From the way he kissed, I think Brett would've been more than plenty in bed without her having to look elsewhere.

If I was Brett and my sister died, I'd want to be put on her case. That's assuming he worked with the police or FBI. But why wouldn't he have his badge, and why would he be working as a dancer?

Candi came over and was chatting away. She was finishing a conversation we had started a couple of months ago. I couldn't concentrate on her words. My thoughts kept drifting to Brett.

"Earth to Mars!" Candi waved a hand in my face then giggled. "Earth to Mars . . . that's funny!"

"Huh?"

"I was asking what color you want," she said.

"Oh, you pick it out."

"What's the occasion?"

"Nothing, really. I just needed a pedicure. I do have a date tonight, but I don't think he cares what my toes look like."

"Oh, believe me, they care," she stated. "Guys may not pay attention to much, but when it comes to sexy toes, they get a charge from them."

"Sure, if you say so."

"I'm going to sexify your toes and you can call me tomorrow and tell me I was right."

"Deal," I agreed, knowing I'd never have to make the call.

I lounged back, watching Candi work. She was a perfectionist when it came to nails. Everything had to be trimmed, filed, buffed, and perfectly polished. Only then would she let you leave the chair.

"You need to come and see me more often," Candi urged. "You've been abusing your feet."

"How can you tell?" I asked. "They look fine to me."

"They're not fine," she insisted. "You have rough and dry feet, a callous, and your nails aren't evenly shaped."

"I didn't realize they were that bad."

She rubbed lotion on my feet and legs. It's a good thing I shaved not too long ago.

"Have you ever considered becoming a massage therapist?" I asked.

"I've been told I have a nice, firm touch, but I like nails."

"If you ever decide to switch, I'll be your first client."

I relaxed and let Candi work her magic. My eyes closed and a wave of exhaustion passed over me.

* * *

A hand pressed on my shoulder. "Mars," Candi said.

My eyes blinked open. "Huh? Oh! I must have fallen asleep," I said with a large yawn. My eyes zoomed in on my toes. They were stunning. "Candi, this is amazing!"

"I know. I've been practicing a new technique."

I admired the deep-purple paint. Both large toes were painted to resemble orchids on a Japanese painting. The finished look was tropical and exotic—poetry for toes.

I gave her a hug and moved to the desk to pay for the service. I opened my wallet to find three dollars and change. I mentally smacked my head. I'd forgotten I didn't have any money. Think! My eyes slid to the Viper. A crisp one hundred dollar bill was just sitting in the glove box not getting the love and attention it deserved.

If I took the money, I'd be at the mercy of Brett, my brain tried to reason. I really didn't have an option at this point, however. I took a deep breath, told the girl at the register I'd be right back, and heisted the money out of the car. A sticky note on the back of the bill caught my attention.

Mars, just use it. – Brett

It's scary how he can predict me.

I paid the girl at the register and walked back to the Viper, careful to avoid damaging the goods that might cost me dearly later.

Maybe he wouldn't notice the money was missing. I could sneak the money back into the glove box. It might work, but knowing Brett, he probably knows the c-number of the bill. There'd be no way I could get around that. A problem to solve later.

I was near the jewelry store, so I called Jonathan for an update on the lockets.

"Hi, Jonathan," I greeted when he answered. "How are the lockets coming along?"

"I'm almost done," he replied. "Why don't you come and take a look? I'm on my last couple. It won't take me long to finish."

"I'm right around the corner. I'll see you in a couple of minutes."

Jonathan was busy at his small work desk. The desk lamp was turned on as he worked with his engraver. The little tool made sounds that reminded me too much of the dentist, and I wished I had waited before coming.

Jonathan acknowledged me with a nod then bent his head down to finish the locket. He had each locket in its own little box sitting on the counter for me to inspect. I trusted Jonathan completely, but he liked to make sure his work was inspected and approved before anything left his store.

I ran a finger over one of the heart-shaped lockets. It was crafted out of sterling silver and had a small sapphire stone in the middle. On the back, it was engraved with Jonathan's steady hand.

He didn't just write in block letters; it looked like formal script. The letters flowed in the tiny space. He was a genius with the engraver. The lockets were made to be worn either on a chain for a necklace or bracelet, or they could be put on a key chain. We would have the necklaces and key chains available at the party for the guests to choose.

Jonathan finished the last locket and brought it to the counter. "What do you think?"

"They're perfect," I replied.

He smiled with satisfaction. He closed the boxes and placed them in a bag.

"Should I charge them to the account?"

"Yes, please," I said. "Thanks again for making them so fast."

"Anytime," he said. "Don't forget to take the promotional cardboard cutout to plug the store at the dinner."

"What cardboard cutout?"

He pointed over to the corner where a life-size poster cutout of Jonathan stood. He was dressed in a pinstriped suit and was holding a tray that overflowed with jewelry. A sign at the bottom announced: Need pleasure? Buy treasure.

"Wow! Uh . . . that's, um, nice. Are you sure you want me to take it?" I asked him.

"You did say you were going to plug the store."

"I was thinking something smaller . . . like business cards."

Jonathan pursed his lips and crossed his arms over his chest.

"Okay." I gave in, not wanting to offend. "I'll take the cutout of you."

He smiled.

I'll have to put it in a corner where no one will see it.

I carried the bag of lockets and the cutout of Jonathan to the car. Now I just needed to pick up the pictures Curtis had ordered. I shoved cutout Jonathan to the passenger's side.

I smiled as the Viper purred down the street. Testosterone car, drop-dead gorgeous man, and money in the glove box; a girl could get used to this. I peered over at cutout Jonathan and groaned.

It didn't take long for the cashier to find the photo order and bill it to the company account. I peeked at the photos before I left. It'd take me forever to cut these to the right shape and place them into the lockets. I'm a numbskull for trying this with hardly any time to spare.

I gazed down at the young woman and man in the photo. They looked like they had the whole world ahead of them. Now they're in their eighties and looking back at the world. I thought about the two men who had snuck into my life: one man I can't get a straight answer from, and the other man has a short attention span.

I drove back to the office and parked. I hope Emmy can help with the lockets.

Jocelyn was on her way out. "Mars, did you ever get the number for that dancer at Longhorn's? He hasn't been there the last couple of nights."

"Uh, no," I muttered. "It's against company policy to give out a dancer's phone number."

"That's no good. Did you tell them we're clients and need his phone number?"

"They said you can leave a message for him and they'd make sure he gets it."

Her eyes perked. "Well, then," she oozed. "I'll go over there right now." Jocelyn turned to her car but paused before she stepped in. "Who's car is that?"

"I'm borrowing it from a friend until mine is repainted."

"I've seen that car before at Longhorn's. Who does it belong to?"

"Um, well, funny story," I tried to laugh, but only a strangled sound came out.

"I don't have time for a story," she said, tapping her dagger nails on her BMW roof.

"Oh, well, too bad," I said.

Her brown eyes glared. "You should have work done on your eyes," she said. "You're looking dreadful. I have a reputation to uphold. I can't have ugly people working for me." And with that, Jocelyn peeled out of the parking lot, leaving me to inhale her exhaust.

I walked into the office. "Emmy, do I look dreadful to you?"

She tilted her head. "I wouldn't say dreadful. But you seem stressed and it's giving you dark circles under your eyes."

I pulled out my compact mirror and inspected my eyes. Dark, crescent-shaped moons only my dad would love were sucking up serious territory under my eyes.

"Emmy, what am I going to do?" I asked. "I have a date tonight."

"Hmm, not to worry. Now that Jocelyn's gone for the day, we can fix you up."

Emmy snatched the phone and called her cousin Desiree.

"Desiree will be here in ten minutes," she informed me. "She's a student at the beauty school and has been bugging me to find her someone to practice on."

"Desiree knows what she's doing, right?" I asked.

"Of course. She's been through two weeks already. She's done amazing things with my mom."

"Okay. I guess I can't look any worse."

I handed the bag of lockets and photos to Emmy. "Will you be able to help me with these?"

"Sure. Why don't we start now and see how many we can get done. Curtis could probably help, too," she said, buzzing Curtis to come to the front.

Curtis stalled when he spied the lockets and photos spread out on Emmy's desk. His eyes flicked toward me. "Tell me you didn't!"

"I thought it'd be a good idea," I said. "If you don't have time, I can do them tonight and tomorrow. I should be able to finish in time."

"No," he sighed. "I can help. I'm almost finished with the list anyway. Everything else can be done tomorrow."

Curtis pulled up a chair. We cut and inserted pictures into the lockets. After the first couple, a growing ache started in my neck and a cramp developed in my hand. I decided to stretch and retrieve the cardboard cutout from the car.

When I returned, Curtis blinked with wide eyes. I could see his lips moving as he read the sign.

He arched his brow. "What is that?"

"I told Jonathan we would plug the store if he could get the lockets to us in time."

"Did you ever think about getting business cards from the guy?"

I slid him a narrow glance and set Jonathan near the back wall.

Desiree pranced through the door with her beautician's tackle box. She looked the part. Her makeup was a little heavy but perfectly executed. Her bleach-blonde hair was styled and clipped. She wore tight, colorful clothes that showed off her perky breasts, which matched her perky attitude.

"Hi," she said, beaming. "Who's going to be my victim?"

Did she have to use that word?

"Do you have time to get us all in?" Emmy asked.

Desiree jumped up and down like she'd won a year's supply of makeup.

"Yes!" she exclaimed. "Emmy, I'll start with you. You have big pores that need some help."

She pulled Emmy's honey-blonde hair into a ponytail and draped a towel around her neck, clipping it in the back. "I'll take off your makeup first," she informed Emmy.

I watched for a little while, but the lockets weren't going to finish themselves. I picked up the scissors and started snipping.

Snipping the pictures of the happy couple was getting to me. Thoughts raced through my head that normally weren't a concern. What if I never get married? Will I be happy by myself? I figured I'd have to be. I'm not married now and I'm happy. Men don't secure happiness. If anything, they tend to do the opposite. I pondered some of the great tragic romances like Romeo and Juliet, Rhett and Scarlett, and Bonnie and Clyde. I wonder if Rhett ever returned to Scarlett.

Emmy relaxed with cucumbers on her eyelids. Desiree threw a towel over Curtis, wrapping it around his neck.

"I have dry skin, but watch out for my T-zone. It's oilier than a greased-up mechanic. Oh, and I have a date tonight, so make my skin glow," he said.

"Mars, you never said who you were going out with tonight," Emmy said. "Is it Evan?"

"No, it's not Evan," I answered.

"You can forget it," Curtis mumbled under the warm towel Desiree had draped across his face. "I already tried to figure it out earlier; she's as bristly as my Aunt Giddy's five o'clock shadow." He peeked out from his towel. "But she's driving his Viper. It's parked outside."

Emmy sat straight up, peeling the cucumbers off her blue eyes to look out the window. "It must be the other guy."

"What?" I looked up from the locket.

"You're seeing the other guy," she said with a smirk. "My cousin saw you bring in a hot guy to the hospital right before you completely made out with Evan only a few minutes later."

I groaned. Curtis sucked in air, flinging off his towel to gape.

I should have known. Emmy has about a hundred cousins that all live and work in the city. She conveniently has a family network of spies. We've worked together so long that they all know me, but it's impossible for me to know all of them. I only have a dozen memorized.

"Was your cousin at the front desk?"

"Yes." Emmy said with a laugh. "I've been dying to ask you about it!"

I didn't say anything.

"You at least have to tell me about Evan," she insisted, and Curtis nodded his head in agreement. "I imagine he could make a girl weak in the knees. He's always getting girls left and right, so he has to have something other than just looks. How was the kiss?"

"I was waiting for Brett in the hospital. That's the other guy," I explained. "Evan saw me in the waiting room and wanted me to walk him back to the truck, and then he kissed me. It was perfectly innocent."

"It wasn't perfectly innocent according to the description my cousin gave."

"Fine. He made me weak in the knees . . . happy?"

Desiree sighed, wrapping a towel around my neck. "I'd give anything to have a man make me feel that way," she said. "The guys I go out with have a one-track mind. It's always to their satisfaction, never to mine." She dabbed some white stuff on my face.

"I can guarantee Evan has a one-track mind too. He's just excellent along the way," I replied.

"I wish Evan was playing for the other team," Curtis said. "His blue eyes make me sweat."

I blushed under the white junk. My face tingled. "Is this stuff supposed to tingle?" I asked.

"I'm not sure," Desiree said. She read the bottle and worry spread across her face. "Perhaps we should take it off."

She blotted most of it off and then placed a cool washcloth on my face to wipe off the rest.

Curtis gawked.

"What?"

"Uh, well, it'll be okay . . . I think," Desiree muttered, digging through her box. "I'm sure I have something in here that will help."

The sound of screeching tires made us stop and turn toward the window. A barrage of bullets shattered the window, screaming through it.

"Get down!" I bellowed.

Chapter 9

We dropped to the floor as an onslaught of bullets terrorized the back wall. The attack stopped nearly as fast as it had started. The car peeled out of the parking lot and raced down the street, leaving us with an eerie silence that made my skin crawl with uncertainty and fear.

"What the hell just happened?" Curtis shrieked.

"Is everyone okay?" I asked louder than I meant to. The deafening sound of the gun and shattering glass left my ears numb.

My eyes shot around the room. The front window was gone except for a few shards still wedged in the frame. Bullet holes riddled the back wall, filing cabinets, desks, and the cutout of Jonathan.

Curtis grasped his chest and hyperventilated behind a desk. Desiree, pale faced, fell in next to him.

"Emmy?" I asked.

There wasn't a response. I ran to her desk and peered behind it. Emmy was sprawled on her back, unconscious. I checked for blood, but I couldn't find any. She must have fainted again.

I yanked a paper bag out of the cabinet for Curtis to breathe into and then called the police. We huddled on the floor, waiting for what seemed like an hour, but in all likelihood it was closer to five minutes.

A wailing ambulance pulled in first, followed by the police.

Evan and his partner, Gordy, rushed inside. Gordy ran to Curtis and Desiree and assisted them. Evan fixed his eyes on me before kneeling beside Emmy.

A second ambulance pulled in. Evan released Emmy into their care. I held my breath as he turned and walked toward me.

"Are you okay?" He looked into my eyes, searching for signs of shock.

"I'm fine," I said.

"What happened to your face?"

I touched my face. I had completely forgotten about it.

Desiree was on the brink of tears. "I don't know," she cried, handing Evan the bottle. "I put this on her and she said her face tingled."

"Come with me," Evan said. "You may have a chemical burn."

He wrapped his hand on my upper arm to help me to the ambulance. I inhaled a sharp breath as a shock ran through me. Evan quickly released me and inspected my arm. Tears streaked down my face. The salt in the tears stung my face and I cried more.

"You're okay," Evan reassured me. "Come to the truck and I'll get you fixed up."

He put his arm around my waist, steered me to the truck, and helped me inside. He sat me down and cut the sleeve off my shirt. Blood trickled down my arm. My stomach took a giant leap.

"It's just a flesh wound. Look at something else if it bothers you," he said.

I took his advice and looked at him. He worked quickly. He must have been very gentle, because I didn't feel him clean the wound or put the bandage on.

He caught me looking at him and smiled. "Penny for your thoughts."

"You'd need a whole lot more than a penny to get these thoughts."

After my arm, he inspected my face.

"My face hurts," I said. "Please, don't tell me what I look like. I'm afraid to know."

"You're still beautiful," he reassured me. "Just really red."

"Red is normal for me."

Evan smiled. "This shouldn't sting," he said as he applied ointment. It immediately cooled my skin. His fingers were gentle on my face . . . slow and lingering. Could he be a gentle lover?

Get your mind out of the gutter!

Evan kissed the top of my head. "Better?"

"Yeah, it feels better," I said.

"Keep this on your face and reapply every few hours," he said, handing me the tube of ointment.

"Thanks, Doc." I smiled.

"I'm not a doctor yet," he said softly. "But for you, I'll be anything you want."

Yikes!

"Let me give you a ride home and I can take care of you for the rest of the night."

My head said, "Yes, please!" But my mouth said, "Thanks, but I have a car that someone loaned me. I need to return it."

"The Viper?" he asked calmly, but there was a hard look in his eyes.

"Yeah, how did you know?"

"Never mind," he said. "Just be careful."

Evan pulled me into a hug. His arms were strong and warm. Everything seemed right until he let go and opened the door to let me out.

"I'll see you soon, sugar," he said, escaping to the front of the truck and sliding in. Gordy hopped in on the passenger's side.

Evan drove away.

A rock formed in my throat.

Jocelyn screeched into the parking lot and jumped out of her car.

"What happened? Curtis called and said someone shot the window."

"He's inside. I need to leave."

"What about the window? Who's going to fix it?"

"There's a phonebook on Emmy's desk. I'm sure you'll be fine."

"I demand you stay until the window gets fixed."

"I've been shot, and my face is on fire. I'm going home."

I trudged to the car. Five days ago my life was normal and predictable. Now, I'm on a roller-coaster ride of emotions and dodging bullets. I practiced breathing exercises as I drove home. My face grew hot from the burn. I could see a little of my face in the rearview mirror. It was violently red under the ointment. Tonight was going to be a disaster.

A question swirled in my mind. Who shot the window . . . and why?

I parked in the driveway and looked across the street at Mrs. Janowski. She must have heard the news from headquarters. She was decked out in her husband's old army gear. The army-green shirt hung to her knees, and the pants pooled and wrinkled over her gigantic combat boots. She topped off the look with a helmet three sizes too big. Her grandson's paintball gun rested in the crook of her arm. I gave her a wave. She returned a salute. A small laugh escaped and I shook my head. Even with all of her quirks, I liked having Mrs. Janowski as my neighbor.

I let myself into the front door and locked the deadbolt on the world . . . at least for now. I ran to the bathroom and peered in the mirror. A blotchy, red face stared back at me. I departed the bathroom gloomy.

I wasn't going out like this. Brett would have to reschedule with my dad or go without me. I peeked at the living room clock. He should arrive in an hour. I'll call him and tell him not to come over.

Something wasn't right about the room . . . something was different. My eyes opened round like an owl's. Everything was picked up and put away. My living room walls were painted a beautiful neutral sand color. It actually complemented my décor. Brett had said it would be fixed, but I hadn't believed him. This room looked better than it did before the break-in.

I found Brett's number on my caller ID and dialed. Butterflies zoomed around my stomach. I had never actually called his phone number before. My call was sent straight to voicemail. I breathed a sigh of relief; voicemail can't argue with you.

"Hi, Brett," I spoke to the voicemail. "It's Mars. I have to cancel tonight. I've had a bit of a . . . well, let's just say issue. Thanks for letting me use your car and for having my place cleaned and painted; it looks beautiful." I hung up, smacking the heel of my hand to my forehead. "OW!"

I hauled myself upstairs to change. I pulled out a camisole and shorts. I may as well be comfortable. I drenched a washcloth with ice-cold water and plopped down on the couch in front of the television. I flipped through the stations and groaned. Why do I pay for hundreds of channels when there's never anything on?

The romance channel was showing The Sound of Music. Good enough. I put the remote control down, reclined back, and tossed the washcloth over my face. The nuns were singing about Maria.

I should join a convent.

Some minutes later, Maria was sent to the Von Trapp family, and I heard a car pull into my driveway. I didn't bother getting up. I wasn't about to answer the door for anyone.

I heard a knock on the door, and then the doorbell rang. After a few more moments, I didn't hear anything. Good, they must have left.

"Why didn't you answer the door?" Brett simmered in my ear.

I rocketed up, kicking the end table with my bare toe.

"Shit!" I cried in agony. Tears pooled in my eyes and burned as they streaked down my face for the second time.

Brett stared at my bottom as I bent over to rub my toe. I didn't care if my cheeks were hanging out of my shorts; my poor toe was in agony.

"You need to sit down," Brett said, wrenching his eyes away.

His hand closed around my waist, pulling me down to the sofa. He touched the tip of my chin, directing my face to his. He then glanced at my bandaged arm.

"What happened?" he asked. His face set with a look of concern.

"It's a long story," I said, still rubbing my toe. "Didn't you get my message?"

"Yes, I heard it. You didn't say you were hurt. I assumed you were avoiding me."

"Am I able to do that?" I asked.

"No."

"I didn't think so. How did you get in here?"

"I still have your key."

"Oh," I said, amazed I didn't really care.

"Does your face hurt?" he asked while inspecting.

"A little. The washcloth helps," I replied.

"Then put it back on and relax."

"What about you?"

"I'll rub your toe," he said.

Brett placed my feet on his lap. I dropped my head down on the pillow, draping the washcloth on my face.

"What happened to your arm?" he asked while massaging my foot.

"I was shot."

His hand stopped.

"They were a lousy shot." I said. "It sounded like they fired off a hundred rounds, and out of the four of us, I was the only one shot. Well, Jonathan didn't make it but that's probably for the best. Evan said I only had a flesh wound."

"Evan?"

"Yeah, you know, Evan West the E.M.T."

"Yeah, I know."

I moved the washcloth to peek at him. He looked surly.

"I can't help who gets called to the scene. Aren't you supposed to be concerned over who shot me instead of who bandaged the wound?"

Brett's face relaxed, "You're right. Let me make it up to you."

Brett massaged my foot. The pain dulled as his fingers massaged and caressed.

"Who's Jonathan? I'm sorry he died."

"Jonathan is a ridiculous cardboard cutout. I'm thankful he's the one that got shot."

"I thought he was a person."

"He is a person, but it's his cutout that was riddled with bullets."

Brett's thumb circled over a pressure point and pressed down.

"Oh!"

He grinned and pressed down just a little deeper. My back arched. Each time he touched a point, a sensual need rolled through my body. Was this payback for bringing up Evan? If that's the case, I'll mention him every hour.

He moved to the other foot, finding just the spot to send vibrations through my core.

"You should probably stop," I said, holding my breath.

"I really shouldn't."

He pulled the washcloth from my face to watch my expression as he raised my foot. He smirked right before he lowered his mouth, kissing each toe. He traced the most sensitive spots of my foot with the tip of his tongue.

"Oh . . ."

Sensations that haven't been explored for a long time—and some that I've never experienced—were swirling rapidly toward release. He brushed his finger over a spot that sent me into a state of blissful agony and near the verge of overload.

"You can stop now," I begged weakly.

He moved his thumb a fraction over and pressed firmly. My breath caught as a wave rolled through me. I grabbed the pillow from under my head, shoving it into my face just before . . .

"OMIGOD!"

My body released all its energy with an uncontrollable shudder, and I sank heavily into the couch.

Holy crap! He just gave me the best orgasm of my life by playing with my feet.

I pulled the pillow down to look at him with wide eyes, not believing what had just happened.

"I couldn't help it," he smirked. "Your toes are sexy as hell."

"I'm glad you like them," I said, trying to regulate my breath. "You paid for them."

He eyed me in wonder. I must have passed whatever test he was giving because he growled, "That makes it even sexier."

I rested my head back on the pillow, covering my face with the washcloth. Damn, I'll have to call Candi tomorrow . . . maybe I'll send her a gift basket.

"Did you study reflexology?" I asked.

"It's just one of my many talents," he said.

Brett set my feet on the couch as he moved out from under me and slid to settle on top. He removed the washcloth and propped himself up with his elbows to study my face. He winced in pain from his cracked rib but didn't bother to move. His hard body pressed heavily on me.

"I could show you more upstairs," he said.

"I'll take a rain check," I said as I halfheartedly tried to push him off.

He bent his head down. His lips touched mine. His mouth was soft and lingering. Perhaps it's good that I'm staying home. I wanted more of his lips, his kiss, and . . . him.

"Are you ready to go?" he asked.

"Hmm?"

"To go to your dad's house." He kissed the valley between my breasts using just a hint of tongue that drove me back on edge.

"I'm not going," I said.

"Yes, you are," he said, pulling me to my feet.

"I'm not going," I repeated. From an early age, stubbornness ran rampant through my veins. It tends to come out when I'm forced to do something I don't want to do—also when I fight my dad for the last piece of dessert.

"I'm injured." I feigned helplessness, hoping to find a compassionate side of Brett.

"You're not so weak as to use that line," he said. Brett scooped me up, flung me over his shoulder, and swung the door open.

"Not again. Brett, put me down. You have the mannerisms of a cave man."

Mrs. Janowski sat on the porch with a smile plastered on her face.

"Mrs. J., shoot him with your gun," I called out.

"It's about time a man whisked you off your feet," she hollered back, giving Brett a salute. "Looks like he has you head over heels, too!" She was tickled pink at her joke and gave her knee a happy slap.

Oh, geez!

"I don't have any shoes, and I can't go in this outfit," I said.

"You won't need shoes, and I like this outfit." Brett grinned.

Brett repositioned me, holding my bottom with one hand while opening the car door with the other. He gently dropped me in. I sulked while Brett angled in on the driver's side and started the car.

"Whose car is that?" I pointed to the red car parked next to us in the driveway.

"It's yours."

"My car is blue," I said.

"It was blue, but now it's red," he said.

"Why red?"

"When they asked me what color I wanted, I said red," he said. "You have a red personality. The blue car didn't suit you."

I didn't argue. If I had money to spend on a car, it'd be red.

"Do you normally go after girls with a red personality?" I asked. I didn't know if he'd give me a straight answer.

He gave a small laugh, "I think that may be a red-personality question. I normally stay away because two strong personalities don't mix well."

"Then why me? You obviously know a lot about me and my personality."

"You were trouble the moment I laid eyes on you, but you've shown me a few extra colors that intrigue me. You may be worth the trouble," he said, adding deviously, "and if not, then we'll have had one hell of a good time anyway."

"What if I'm not looking for trouble?"

"Sweet thing, you were made for trouble."

I could see us going around in circles on that point, so I changed the subject. "By the way, I meant to yell at you for making dinner arrangements with my dad and not even asking me."

"Kind of too late for that."

"I know. I'm just putting it out there."

He reached for my hand, bringing my palm up to his lips. I melted back into the seat and relaxed the rest of the way to my dad's house.

Brett pulled up to the front door of the little yellow house. It was my childhood home and has been yellow since it was built in the seventies. The only thing that changed was the height of the trees.

I didn't ask how Brett found the place without directions. He seemed to know everything; why waste my breath?

"Want me to carry you to the door?"

"Not on your life," I said, fleeing from the car.

The front door swung open before I even climbed the first step on the porch.

"It's about time you two arrived," my mom said as she breezed through the door to get a better view of Brett.

"Mom, what are you doing here?"

"You know how your dad is. He invites people over and then forgets about the food," she said. "He always has his head stuck in space."

Her eyes admired Brett. "Well?" she asked. "Have you forgotten your manners? Aren't you going to introduce us?"

"Oh, sorry," I said. I had been taken by surprise when my mom appeared at the door. She hasn't set foot in the house for a good five years. "Mom, this is Brett. Brett this is my mom, Diane."

"It's very nice to meet you," Brett said.

"It's so nice to meet you, Brett," Mom said, ushering us in the house.

Brett gave me a wink that went unnoticed by my mom. She was currently staring at his biceps.

"Where's Dad?"

"Oh, he's out fiddling with his gadgets."

Mom already had the wine open and was pouring her second glass. She poured a glass for Brett and me.

"I probably shouldn't," I said as she offered the glass.

"One glass won't hurt you," she said.

"One glass is my limit."

"Dear, what happened to your face?"

"My face reacted badly to face cream."

My dad popped in from the backyard. "I thought I heard you arrive." He gave me a kiss on the head. "You look all red. You better watch out for sunburn. Do you know that the surface of the sun is nearly ten thousand degrees Fahrenheit, and the core is about twenty-seven million degrees? Makes you want to wear sunscreen next time, doesn't it?"

I nodded to humor him. "Dad, this is Brett. Brett, this is my dad, Tim."

"Nice to meet you, Brett," my dad said, shaking Brett's hand. "Ready for stargazing?"

"Of course," Brett said.

"After dinner we can go out back and I'll give you a tour of the night sky."

"Sounds good."

I peeked in the kitchen. "Mom, do you need help?" I asked. She wasn't a gourmet by any means, and the apple didn't fall far from the tree.

"I'm almost done," she said as she spooned portions from a white box onto each plate.

"You ordered catering again, didn't you?"

She gave me a knowing smile. "First impressions count," she said. "After a couple times over, and you have him madly in love with you, then I'll bring out my below-average cooking."

"Sounds like you've thought about it."

"Oh, I have, dear. And you're making it easier wearing that little outfit."

"He wouldn't let me change."

"Good for him. I like a man who knows what he wants. Just keep those outfits coming until grandchildren are on the way."

Where's that wine?

Mom and I carried the plates into the dining room and we all took a seat.

Dad eyed the food suspiciously and took a bite. "Diane, this is really good. You've improved."

I smirked and she shot a warning look.

"It's the best home-cooked food I've tasted in a long time," Brett said.

Mom took a gulp of wine.

"So, what do you do for a living, Brett?" she asked.

"I work at Longhorn's."

"Oh, a bartender. A man after my own heart." She raised her wine glass.

"No, I'm a dancer."

Dad stalled with a forkful of food halfway into his mouth. Mom took another gulp of wine.

"You're an exotic dancer?" she asked with a small cough.

"He's really good, too. Got twenty bucks off me his first dance," I said.

Mom choked and Dad's fork hung lifelessly by his lips.

Brett smirked. "Don't worry," he said to my parents, "it's only temporary."

"I guess if you have the looks, you may as well use them," Mom said, taking another gulp of wine. "Those thong things don't cut off circulation, do they? I need grandbabies soon."

"Mom!"

"Diane," Dad said softy, "perhaps you should go easy on the wine."

Mom shrugged and stuck a fork of pasta in her mouth.

The rest of the meal was finished with small talk. I spent the time looking back and forth from Mom to Dad. It was odd to see them sitting at the same table. They didn't seem to find it awkward at all and even bickered like old times.

"Brett, come on back and let me show you the stars," Dad said.

We deposited Mom on the couch. She curled up with her wine glass and a throw blanket.

Dad led the way outside, with Brett and me trailing behind. Brett took my hand in his and we strolled through the backyard.

"Do you know about the power of ten?" Dad asked Brett.

"I can't say that I do."

"It helps to comprehend how big the universe is."

"How so?" Brett asked.

"Let's just say you have ten bananas and you multiply those by ten, it would equal one hundred. But then you multiply again my ten and you get a thousand bananas. If you keep multiplying by ten, you would get ten thousand, then one hundred thousand, then one million, then ten million. Each time you multiply, it would increase drastically and yet you only started out with ten bananas. What do you think of that?"

Brett grinned. "That's a heck of a lot of bananas."

Dad tapped the side of his nose. "Bingo. It's a lot of bananas and a lot of space," he said, giving me the approving nod to signal that Brett had passed his second challenge question.

Dad pulled out his sky map, handing it to Brett. "Sit here," he said, motioning to the Adirondack chairs. "This is a sky map," he explained. "It shows what is viewable in the night sky at this time. Mars, why don't you show him how to use it. I'll make sure your mom is settled in, and then I'll grab the binoculars. We don't need a telescope tonight. I think the sky is going to cooperate with us. Then Brett will have another reason to come back. Everyone loves telescopes."

"Only if the telescope is pointed at you," Brett whispered in my ear. If my face wasn't already red, I'd have blushed.

I took the sky map from Brett. He pulled me over to his chair and onto his lap.

"You have to choose the month we are currently in and then line up what time it is, and there," I pointed, "is the map."

"Point out stars for me," he said. "What are your favorites?"

"I love Orion and the Pleiades," I said. "But you can't always see the Pleiades."

"Then why do you like them?"

"The Pleiades are a group of stars also known as the Seven Sisters," I explained. "Since I never had any sisters, the Seven Sisters became a sort of mystical sisterhood. I know it sounds dumb, but I thought they were out there watching out for me."

Brett was quiet. "No, it's not dumb," he finally said.

A knee-jerk reaction in my stomach knocked the wind out of me. I forgot his sister had died. That's why he's here; he's searching for her killer, and I go on about how I never had one.

"I'm sorry," I said softly, kissing his forehead.

"What are you sorry for?"

"I'm sorry I'm insensitive."

He looked at me, searching my eyes, "Insensitive?"

"I'm also sorry that Eve died."

Brett grew perfectly still. "How did you know?"

"Just like you, I make it my business to know."

His eyes darkened, registering me. I carefully stood up to give him space, but he lowered me back down firmly. His thumb stroked the side of my neck and pulled me in. His mouth, hard and raw with emotion, took possession of mine. He released all of his anger and aggression out through his lips.

His tongue took control, exploring deeply. My mind shut out the world, and I sensed the overwhelming need in him. His hand slid up my shirt, seeking out my breast. He played rough, and I groaned, wanting more. Brett's hand was forceful and his mouth intoxicating. He hardened beneath me. I wanted him. I wanted all of him.

"You kids want something to drink?" Dad called from the kitchen.

I pulled back; I had momentarily forgotten where I was. I looked at Brett, confused.

"Anything would be fine, Tim." Brett called back.

I stood up and moved to the chair next to him.

He slipped his hand in mine and squeezed it. I could sense he was staring at me, but I tried to ignore it and concentrated on thoughts that didn't make me want to rip his clothes off. We were close—too close. If my parents weren't here, we would have had all-out hot, steamy sex in the backyard. It would have been great too. Argh, think of dirty socks!

Dad came out with mugs of coffee since it was getting cooler out. I was beginning to freeze in my camisole and shorts. The coffee was a poor substitute for the warmth of Brett. I clutched the mug with both hands.

Dad chatted about the stars for a good hour. He then proceeded to sing a song that helped students remember the constellations.

Brett was a very attentive student, asking all the right questions. He only strayed for a moment to grab me a blanket from inside. He tucked it around me and gave me a kiss on the head. I was content to sit and listen.

Eventually I nodded off, waking up with a start. "Dad, we need to go," I said. "It's getting really late, and I have work tomorrow."

"Oh, would you look at that," he said, glancing at his glowing watch. "It's way past your bedtime, young lady."

We shuffled back into the house. Mom was passed out on the couch with her wine glass held precariously by a couple of fingers.

"I'll take care of her," Dad said. "You two go ahead and take off."

I gave Dad a kiss on his cheek and said goodnight.

Brett ushered me to the car. I settled in, resting my head back on the seat. I wanted to go home and sleep for twelve hours. Not even Brett could make me stray from those plans. We didn't talk on the way home. It wasn't until he parked in the driveway that he finally spoke.

"Are you okay?" he asked.

"I'm tired, but okay." I said as I yawned. "Why?"

He studied my face, running his fingers through my hair. "I'm afraid I hurt you or scared you."

"I have no idea what you're talking about."

"Tonight, in the backyard, I didn't mean to attack you so aggressively. I'd never do anything to hurt you," he said.

I smiled. "Oh, that."

He looked confused. "You wouldn't look at me afterward."

A devious smile crept on my face. "I didn't want to look at you. I was afraid I might rip your clothes off."

"Jesus!" He slammed his head back into the seat then slid his eyes to me. "I've been agonizing all night because I might have hurt you or scared you off, and you wanted me to finish what I started."

"Yeah, pretty much."

He gave a low laugh and kissed me. "You're beautiful."

He escorted me to the door and let me in. I didn't know if I should ask him in or not. I wanted him to stay, but I desperately needed my sleep, too. Luckily, he made the decision. After giving me a delicious kiss, he headed back to the car.

"I'll be back for more," he threatened.

I climbed the stairs to the bedroom, pulled on a T-shirt, and dove under the sheets. I was floating on a soft, fluffy cloud.

"This isn't my mattress."

I hopped off the bed and peeked under the sheets to find a top-of-the-line pillowtop mattress. I hugged it with adoration. Tonight, I was going to sleep like a queen. Thank you, Brett!

* * *

I awoke to the creaking sound of footsteps downstairs. I grabbed my bat. It may be Brett, but why would he come back so soon? Unless he wanted to finish where we left off.

The footsteps were now on the staircase, creeping up stair by stair. It couldn't be Brett; he wouldn't walk so slowly. The footsteps stopped at my door . . . the handle turned.

Chapter 10

"I'm calling the police!" I shouted. I watched the door handle to see it stop turning.

I dialed Brett instead. I strained to hear footsteps, but I couldn't hear anything past my thundering heart.

"You want me, don't you?" Brett asked as he answered the phone.

"There's someone outside my bedroom door!" I shrieked.

"I'm on my way," Brett said. "Do you have your bat?"

"Yes."

"Good. Stay on the phone with me. Don't hang up."

"Okay," I said bravely. Tears welled at the back of my eyes.

"Can you hear anything?"

"No, it's silent."

Brett asked me frivolous questions to keep me focused. The time ticked away as I stared so hard at the doorknob that my eyes grew dry and weary.

"Brett, I need to get out of here before I go crazy."

"I just pulled into your driveway. Stay in your room. Don't come out, even if you think you hear me. I'll come to you. Do you understand?"

I nodded.

"I can't hear if you nod. Do you understand?"

"Yes."

"I'm going to hang up now. I'll see you in a couple of minutes."

I nodded and hung up.

I listened for signs of Brett while my hands formed a death grip on my bat. A couple of minutes later there was a knock on my door. My stomach lurched and I was paralyzed. There was a knock again.

"It's Brett," he said through the door. "I'm going to open the door. You won't hit me with the bat, will you?"

I shook my head.

"I'm assuming you're shaking your head no. Please, don't hit me with the bat."

Brett nudged the door open and peeked in before he assumed it was safe to let himself in and then shut the door behind him. He was wearing boxer shorts and a gun. Nothing else.

"You can put the bat down now. Whoever was here is gone," he assured me.

I tried to put the bat down but my body stayed rigid. He walked in front of me, placed his hand on mine and slipped the bat out of my hand. With the bat gone, the dam from behind my eyes broke and the tears poured. He wrapped me in his arms, letting me cry on his bare chest until I was sure there wasn't any liquid left in me.

"When I first met you, I told myself I should stay away from you because this might happen," Brett said in my ear. "I don't want you to end up like my sister. But, you seem to be my weakness. I can't stay away from you. I was scared out of my mind that someone was going to take you away from me. Until this ends, I'll be your shadow and stay next to you at all times."

I sniffled and nodded. I couldn't think anymore. I just wanted my pillowtop mattress and to snuggle into Brett. He granted that wish, and I slept soundly in his arms until the morning sun woke me.

* * *

I unwrapped myself from Brett's secure arms and dragged myself into the shower. The warm water beat against my aching muscles, drowning the growing tension. After my skin started to prune, I turned off the water. I wrapped the towel around me and dropped back down to reality when I found a message written in red paint, or what I hoped was red paint, on the outside of my bedroom door.

The chase has just begun. – Hammer.

My heart plummeted. The Hammer was after me, and the town car guys were too.

I looked in at Brett sleeping and remembered what he had said last night. Brett was going to be my shadow. It wouldn't be so bad, would it? I'll think of him as an adorable puppy that can turn into a killer attack dog when needed. But I can't bring puppies to work. He'll just have to find something else to do.

The Mayor's luncheon was set to begin in just a couple of hours. I had to get down to the conference center and help organize the room.

I dressed in jeans and a short-sleeved knit shirt. I packed a skirt, blouse, and heels in a bag to change into right before the lunch. I've been to my fair share of events where I hauled tables and chairs, helped in the kitchen, and fixed whatever inevitably went wrong. Too many dress clothes have been ruined, so now I go in jeans. Nice jeans. I still need to be professional.

I left a note for Brett telling him I had gone to work. I snuck out of the house and slipped into my red car. It didn't seem like my car anymore. Red and shiny wasn't something I normally could afford. I didn't want to know how much I owed Brett for this. I should have asked last night.

* * *

At the conference center, I pulled out my event agenda and checklist. A quick inspection of the room showed me the tables were already set up and the edges of the chairs aligned just right with the edges of the table. I smiled. Perfect.

Curtis and Emmy arrived moments later and we sat down to figure out our game plan.

"Curtis, you take the kitchen and the waitstaff. Emmy, you're on the floor for the guests. I'll take deliveries and the front door for guest arrival," I said.

"No way," Curtis replied. "I had the kitchen last time. I hate working with chefs and their artistic temperament."

I couldn't really argue. Some chefs were born with a great gift for cooking sublime meals. However, more often than not, their temperaments were a bit charred.

I gave them each an agenda and their specific checklists. We each clipped a radio onto our jeans and stuck an earpiece in one ear.

"Test," I said into the radio. Curtis and Emmy radioed their tests. We were good to go. In an hour the room would flood with guests.

Curtis grumbled and left to find the chef. Emmy started on the dining room. I looked for our deliveries. Linens had arrived and were being laid on the tables by the waitstaff. Flowers? Where are the flowers? I pulled out my phone and dialed Flower Power.

"Flower Power. How can I help you?"

"Willow, is that you?" I asked.

"Yes."

"It's Mars. Are the flowers on their way to the conference center?"

"They should be. Hold on a minute. Let me call Kirby and see where he is."

I waited . . . and waited.

"Mars, are you still there? Kirby will be there in about ten minutes. He stopped, um, briefly for something."

I thanked her and hung up. Kirby would be in for a world of hurt if he didn't show up soon. I put him to the back of my mind as the ice sculpture arrived.

Two large men hauled the massive sculpture to the dining room, heaving it gracefully onto a tray that was placed on the table. They surrounded the base with a bed of crushed ice.

The sculpture was a massive bald eagle perched on a log. Behind the eagle was an American flag. I admired it for a little while. It floored me how much work was poured in to this, only for it to be a pool of water by the end of the day. Still beautiful.

"Mars!" Kirby called out, waving to me.

"Where were you?"

"Oh man, I had the most serious case of the munchies."

"I gathered that from the Cheetos dust on your shirt."

"You want some? I got the family bag."

"No, thank you. Let's just get the flowers inside." I stopped, searching his eyes. "You didn't drive while smoking did you?"

"Oh man, I never drive while H.U.I."

"H.U.I.?"

"Happily Under the Influence."

I rolled my eyes and helped him unload his van. I never think I've ordered enough flower arrangements until I have to help haul them in.

After all the flowers were in place, Kirby flashed me the hang-ten sign and left. I looked at the time. Guests should start arriving any moment.

I radioed to Curtis and Emmy. "I'm off the floor to change. Someone watch the door."

Emmy replied a confirmation. I ran to the ladies' room with my bag. I ducked into a stall and stripped off my clothes. The restroom door opened. A guest had already arrived?

I tried to dress faster, but my fingers weren't moving as fast as my brain. A button popped off my blouse. "Shit!" I said, slapping a hand over my mouth. Oh, God. Did I just say "shit" in front of a guest?

The lock on the stall door turned and the door swung open. I gasped.

"You didn't wake me up," Brett said, taking an extra-long glance at my opened shirt.

"And that gives you the right to barge into a ladies' restroom?"

"You know why I'm here."

"Yes, but I have to work. You're cute and everything, but I have to pay my bills. I can't have you hanging around while I'm working."

"Then put me to work."

"You're not dressed for it."

"What do I need?"

"Well," I sighed as I fumbled with my buttons, "if you had black dress pants and a white dress shirt you'd be fine."

"Done," he said, helping me button the rest of my shirt. "I like unbuttoning better."

He left me to finish dressing myself. I quickly regained my composure and walked out to see the first guests arriving.

Emmy greeted them and checked their names off the list. Since it was Mayor Fenwig's luncheon, we had to take precautions about who entered. Only invited guests and their plus ones could come into the dining room. Media had to remain out in the lobby but could later attend the speech.

Brett stepped next to me. He was wearing black dress pants and a white button-down shirt. He even had black leather dress shoes on. I gave him a suspicious stare.

"I'm always prepared," he said with a hint of grin.

I handed him our spare radio. "We keep it on channel one."

I pressed the talk button on my radio. "Curtis and Emmy, Brett is helping us today. He has a radio in case you need him."

Emmy glanced over at us from her position at the front door. She gave a small smile and returned to the guests.

"What do you want me to do?"

"Just smile and help anyone who needs it. Walk the room and be friendly." I stopped. "Not too friendly."

I surveyed the room. Wine and hors d'oeuvres were being served. Excellent timing.

Mayor Fenwig should be arriving soon. I stepped outside to see if I could spot him. The valets raced as fast as they could to keep up with the arriving guests.

A black town car pulled up along the front door; its back window was cracked open. I stepped behind a pole to keep myself out of sight. My stomach dropped to my shoes as Mayor Fenwig and his wife stepped out of the car. I shook my head. It couldn't be them, could it?

They nodded to a few people, shaking hands as they entered. I've never met Fenwig's wife, but she looked familiar. I must have seen her in the newspaper or on television. The town car pulled away. I discreetly followed them.

Brett helped a pretty blonde to her seat. An electric zap hit me between the eyes. I tried to tell myself it wasn't jealousy. He did tell me he doesn't normally go for my type. Maybe he likes the perky pinks or happy yellows. He looked up to see me staring at him. I gave a small jump, realizing he'd caught me in an unpleasant thought and most likely a jealous glare. A hint of a smile escaped his lips and he lingered with the blonde a little longer. Where's Mrs. J.'s paintball gun when you need it?

Emmy called Brett for reinforcement at the front entrance. I searched for Mayor Fenwig and his wife. They were standing with a few other guests, sipping wine. Three fingers worth of wine was poured into each glass. Mrs. Fenwig swallowed it in one gulp and snapped her fingers at the server for more.

The staff was trained to pour three fingers worth of wine and refill as necessary, but with Mrs. Fenwig drinking, we may just hand her the bottle and toss a straw in it. The server poured another serving of wine. She sneered at him, wanting more. He filled her glass until it reached the rim. After she was satisfied, the server passed by me with a startled expression.

Karina Fenwig sipped the top off and surveyed the room. She didn't look like a politician's wife. I always picture them with a skirt suit and perfectly dull hair. She wore a low-cut, dark-blue dress that glittered in the light. Her hair was coarse and dry from all the over styling and bleaching it took to create full-body blonde waves. Her eyeliner looked like it had been caked on for the past twenty years and never once removed.

Karina took another sip and found an object of fascination. I followed her eyes to Brett. She licked her lips, checked her makeup in her compact, and wiggled her expensive boobs into place. Karina whispered into her husband's ear. He smiled and nodded.

Emmy was right on schedule and turned on the microphone so Fenwig's aid could introduce the mayor. There was brief applause while Fenwig made his way to the podium and started his speech. The speech was scheduled to last fifteen minutes, but we gave him an extra five minutes since he loves to talk. More to the point, he loves to hear himself talk.

Karina was on the prowl. She maneuvered over to Brett, catching his eye. He gave her a polite smile and resumed helping Curtis. Karina saddled up next to Brett, placing her arm on his and holding on while whispering into his ear.

I looked around the room. Did anyone else see this? Am I the only one who sees Fenwig's wife hitting on Brett? Curtis noticed. His eyebrow arched and he slid me a glance.

Brett removed his arm from hers. She counter attacked with a flick of her hair and a small laugh. She caught his hand and held it, playing with his fingers while talking to him. Curtis fled the scene.

"What's going on?" I asked Curtis.

"She's making a serious move on Brett," he said. "You need to get in there and protect your man."

"He's not my man," I said. "And even if he was, I want to see how this plays out. I know he's not interested in her."

Curtis arched his brow and turned to the kitchen to make sure lunch was on schedule.

I watched Brett and Karina for a moment longer. A spark of recollection hit me.

I remember!

Karina had done the same thing to Jesse Corbin at a different event. The event wasn't for Mayor Fenwig, but they were in attendance. At the time, I had figured they were close acquaintances. Karina must have a thing for luring men at events. Could she have anything to do with Jesse's death?

Brett gave me a look that begged for help. I gave him a small finger wave and a crooked smile. I'll make him talk to her. She may tell him something important.

Crash!

The mayor took no notice of the heart-stopping sound and continued his speech. I rushed to the kitchen. My blood pressure peaked.

Please, don't be the food!

I plowed through the kitchen door and froze to see the chef standing over Curtis. The chef's eyes were slits, his mouth curled with disgust. He threw his hands up in the air, cursing at Curtis who was lying in a pile of food and broken dishes.

I winced and hurried to Curtis. "Are you okay?"

He nodded but his eyes betrayed that he was mortally embarrassed.

"Get your people out of here!" Chef bellowed.

I pulled Curtis up and out of the food and sent him to the back restroom to clean up as best he could. I glanced at Chef but he was in no mood for apologies. I fled the kitchen, retreating out to the floor. I've learned the hard way that chefs can be in a good mood before and after events, but never cross them while they're plating up.

Karina sat at her table just as Fenwig finished his speech. There was a polite round of applause as he finished and joined his wife at the table.

Chef must have used all his tricks because a slew of servers walked out of the kitchen carrying plates of food with silver lids on top. It took twenty minutes to serve everyone and refill wine and water glasses.

I didn't see Curtis return, so I headed through the lobby to go around back the long way. I wasn't about to enter the kitchen. I stopped when I saw Brett. His jaw was clenched. Another woman had found her way to him. Only this woman was Jocelyn. I let out an audible sigh. Jocelyn turned around to see me. Brett breathed a little easier with the distraction.

"Mars, darling!" Jocelyn cooed. "You didn't tell me you hired Brett," she said, squeezing Brett's arm like a rattlesnake.

"Uh, it was a surprise," I told her. "I do need him now, though. Curtis had an accident in the kitchen. I need Brett to go into the men's restroom and make sure he's okay."

"Oh, sure," Jocelyn said, turning to Brett. "You go ahead. I'll be right here waiting for you." She gave him a wink.

Brett, relieved to be called off the floor, took off at a fast pace.

"Get me some wine, won't you?" It wasn't a question.

"Sure, why not."

When I returned with her wine, I asked, "Do you know Karina?"

"Fenwig's wife? Yeah, I've come across her before."

"Did you know she was seeing Jesse Corbin from Longhorn's?"

"Mm-hmm." Jocelyn acknowledged, sipping her wine. "She met him at an event. She has a thing for younger men. I've heard some really kinky rumors floating around about her at Longhorn's."

"Like what?"

"You know, like sex videos and stuff."

"Does her husband know?"

Jocelyn shrugged, gulping the last of her wine. "I don't know. I don't pay too much attention to that stuff." She casually glanced to see if Brett had returned.

"It may take him a while. Curtis was a real mess," I told her. "Why don't you go home for the day? Brett will be at another event."

"Hmm. Maybe I will go home. I don't want to seem too eager. That always drives a man away," she said. "But he will be mine by the weekend. Make sure he is at every event we have." Jocelyn tossed her hair back and strutted out.

I peered into the dining room. The guests were eating and enjoying themselves. The waitstaff was doing an excellent job. Compliments were flying about the food. I wish every event went this smoothly. Even Curtis's little mishap hadn't set us back.

I radioed Emmy to tell her she was on her own and snuck into the women's restroom. I had to go an hour ago, but there never seems to be a good time. I took an extra moment to look at myself in the mirror before I returned to the floor.

My hair had gone limp and my lipstick was faded. I tossed my hair upside-down, attempting to get a little volume. I reapplied a touch of lipstick. The redness from the face-cream burn had already calmed down to a slight pink hue.

As I left the restroom, a hand grabbed me, yanking me into a small cloakroom.

"You're in so much trouble," Brett barked.

I smiled and gave him the most innocent eyes I could muster.

"Damn you!" he exclaimed. "I can't even get mad at you for throwing me to the wolves."

"You're a big, strong man. You can take it," I said with a pause, "and I wanted to see what Karina wanted from you."

"She wanted a whole lot of me that I'm not giving away."

"She and Jesse must have been together," I told him. "I think she is part of this whole mess somehow. I witnessed her do the same thing to Jesse that she did to you. Do you think she's the Hammer? Jesse died from a sledgehammer. Maybe she used him and disposed of him?"

"She's not the Hammer."

"How can you know that?"

"The Hammer only kills women, not men."

"Maybe the Hammer wants to diversify and killed men too. And someone is under the impression you have something of his. Do you have whatever it is they are looking for?"

Brett looked puzzled for a moment. "I do have something. Jesse gave it to me the night he died. That may explain a few things."

"What things?"

"Are you squeamish at all?"

"Only with bugs and snakes."

"I'll show you when we get home."

"Home?"

Brett smiled. "Yes, home." He kissed my bottom lip. "I'm your shadow, remember?"

My pulse raced. I forgot about tonight. Last night was a comfort being in his arms, but tonight . . . I can't even ponder it without getting flushed.

He grazed my neck and shoulders with his lips.

"You taste like vanilla," he said appreciatively.

Brett's nimble fingers worked fast and the cool air-conditioned air seeped into my opened blouse. His warm hand filled the shirt as he expertly found his way, tucking his hand into my bra. I moaned.

"This is only the beginning. There's much more to come," Brett said.

He backed me into the corner. His eyes ravenously looked down at my open blouse and lacey push-up bra.

"God, you're intoxicating," he growled.

If I was intoxicating then he was all out inebriating. My knees weakened. Brett lifted me, settling me down on a small cabinet near the back of the room. My skirt rose precariously high to my hips, and he gained closer access. He fitted his body between my thighs. His swift movements caused me to jump, but he held me in place.

"I don't think so," he said into my neck.

His lips left a trail of heat on my skin as his onslaught of kisses advanced lower. He snapped my bra open. My eyes widened.

"I need to get back to the floor."

"Then tell me to stop," Brett said.

I opened my mouth, but nothing came out. His lips curled into a devilish smile.

Brett narrowed his gaze onto my freshly exposed breasts. "You're killing me, Mars," he said right before he captured my nipple with a graze of his teeth.

A spark of desire hit me below the belt. I grasped his arms to steady myself as he sucked gently. My head fell back and my fingers dug into his arms. Brett slipped his hands up my thighs and then up to my skirt to raise it even higher, exposing my lace panties that dipped right above the Promised Land. He moaned at the sight.

"You did that on purpose," he whispered, biting my earlobe. "You're trying to drive me insane."

I wasn't, but I was relieved to find him in the same state I was.

My radio popped off the back of my skirt and fell to the floor.

"Mars!" Emmy scolded me over the radio. "Your radio was on!"

Uh-oh! I must have been sitting on the radio button. Curtis and Emmy had heard everything from the last couple of minutes. I flashed an evil eye at Brett. A dreamy little smile formed on his face.

"What am I going to do? Oh, this is bad . . . really bad."

He picked up the radio, "Emmy and Curtis, sorry about the little show. We'll be out after Mayor Fenwig gives his final speech."

Brett turned off both radios and looked over at me. I already had my skirt pulled back down and my bra re-clasped.

"Don't you dare," I warned.

"Mars, we'll finish this one way or the other."

"I choose the other . . . but later," I negotiated, trying to button my shirt. I didn't really choose later, but if it got me out of now, I'd take it.

Brett pushed my hands away, helping me re-button. He kissed me on the forehead before letting me escape. I quickly peeked in the mirror and ran my fingers through my hair to straighten it out as best I could.

Dessert had been served, and Fenwig stood up from the table to give his final speech.

Emmy took me aside. "What was that about?"

I flushed. "I don't want to talk about it."

"Oh, no you don't! You can't make out in my ear and then tell me don't want to talk about it."

"I don't know what's happening. I just met Brett. Evan and Brett both seem to be on the prowl, and I've been trying not to become a hussy in the process. But it's not working. I'm about ready to attack both of them."

"No one is going to accuse you of being a hussy. You haven't had a guy in a long time. Just think of it as making up for lost time."

"Yeah, but why are they both coming after me now?"

"Maybe you're letting off pheromones. I read about them."

"Do they taste like vanilla?"

"Vanilla?"

"Never mind. Let's get to the front door so we can usher everyone out of here smoothly."

We waited at the front door. Brett must be standing behind me. His energy radiated, making my skin erupt in tingles. Emmy looked over at him, giving him a knowing smile.

"Where is Curtis?" I asked Emmy.

"He said he would come and help us with the cleanup. He wasn't about to come out here; he's a mess."

I nodded.

The black town car pulled in front of the door and idled. I tried to peer inside at the driver, but I couldn't see anything.

"Emmy, go tell the driver that Mayor Fenwig will be done with his speech in about five minutes. See if he has a tarantula tattoo on his neck."

With a curious expression, Emmy walked over to the town car. I could see her talking to him. She smiled and laughed. Did she just write down her phone number?

"She looks like she's doing just fine over there," Brett said.

"She's giving her phone number to the guy who shot at us. It's most definitely not fine."

Brett spun me around. "You didn't tell me that he's the one who shot at you."

"I didn't actually see him, but I assume it is. Tarantula-tattoo Man has been driving the man threatening me. Mayor Fenwig drove up in the same kind of car with the back window cracked open exactly like the other one. I have a bad feeling about the driver Emmy is talking to."

Emmy bestowed a final smile to the driver and hurried back to us.

"Well? Does he have a tattoo?" I asked her.

"Yes, he does," she said. "He's kind of cute in a bad-boy way. We have a date on Saturday."

I never considered Emmy as a lover of the bad-boy type, but he's the real deal on bad boys. This isn't good.

"Saturday is the wedding. You'll be working," I said

"I'm a guest too. He'll be my plus one."

Tarantula Man was going to be a plus one? If I wasn't terrified of him, I might actually be amused by the idea.

"Just be careful. He's involved with something that's even bigger than he is."

"He is big, isn't he?" Emmy giggled. She was off in la-la land.

I looked at Brett for help. He just shrugged with his hands in his pockets. This was my shadow and protector—not a flicker of worry. Jeez!

Mayor Fenwig finished his speech and a small round of applause erupted in the dining room. Emmy and I took our places at the door as the guests filtered out.

"Thank you for coming," we said, smiling to the departing guests. "Have a wonderful afternoon."

Fenwig and his wife followed the guests out.

"Your speech was marvelous, Mayor," I said as he left.

"Thank you," he said without acknowledging me. He paused for a moment and turned to look at me again. There was a flicker of recognition. He suppressed it, exiting through the door. His wife tucked a piece of paper into Brett's pocket on the way out.

"What was that?" I asked out of the corner of my mouth.

"Her phone number."

Emmy and I said good-bye to the last guest, closing the doors behind them.

"Curtis, you can come out now," I said into the radio.

"This will actually be an easy cleanup," I said to Emmy and Brett. "The conference center has their own staff, so they'll take care of the dishes, tables, and chairs. We just need to remove anything that doesn't belong to them."

Curtis schlepped into the dining room. This was a man who couldn't stand a spot on his shoes and here he was covered in sauces, bits of meat, and vegetables. A funny smell came from his direction. I suppressed a laugh.

Curtis glared at me. "Don't laugh. I feel so gross I could just die. I'll have to burn these clothes."

"I didn't laugh," I said, trying to control myself. "Just go home; there isn't that much to do anyway. The three of us can take care of it."

He whimpered as he made his way to the door. "You could have told me that before I sat in the bathroom like this," he said as he walked out. He held his arms out, afraid to touch himself.

"Emmy, can you take all the glass vases and put them at the front door for Kirby to pick up? The staff can have the leftover flowers. Brett, help me with the linens. We have to bag them and haul them to the back door."

Brett and I stuffed the bags full of linens and heaved them to the back door. It was nice to work with him. He did everything so effortlessly and never broke a sweat. I, on the other hand, looked like I had barely escaped a hurricane. I was damp with perspiration.

Brett picked up a leftover daisy and tucked it into my cleavage. "For later," he said.

* * *

On our way out of the conference center, I turned to Emmy. "How are the lockets coming along? Should I pick them up and bring them home to work on?"

"There are a lot left. I can work on some tomorrow before the dinner, but I won't be able to finish them all."

"I'll go pick them up and work on them tonight at home."

"No, you won't," Brett interrupted.

"Why?"

"I have to work tonight and you're coming with me."

"I'm not going to Longhorn's," I said, my hands on my hips.

"Yes, you are."

Emmy sidestepped us, turning to leave. "I'll let you guys work this out," she said and fled.

I tapped my foot on the ground. I didn't want to see him dance again. I didn't want to see women shoving money into his shiny thong.

"Don't pout," he said softly, bringing me in for a hug.

"I'm not pouting," I said. "I don't see why I have to go with you. What if I go to someone else's house?"

"No, you're staying with me so I can keep an eye on you," he said. "You don't want to see me dance, do you?"

"No," I admitted.

He didn't say anything.

"I can't explain it," I said, searching for the right words.

"You don't have to."

I crawled into my car and he closed the door for me. I should have at least tried to explain. Ugh, who am I kidding? I would have sounded like an idiot. Brett, I can't watch you dance because I'd attack you and have mad, passionate sex with you on the catwalk. Plus, I'd beat the hell out of any woman who even came near you with money. Sure, that would sound great! I hit my head on the steering wheel. "Idiot!"

Brett knocked on my window.

I jumped. "Shit!" I screamed, grabbing my heart. I rolled down the window.

"Are you okay? You seem a little jumpy?" he asked with a smile only a devil could appreciate.

"What do you want?"

"Are you heading over to work to pick up the lockets?"

"Yes."

"I'll follow you. Unless you want to drive together and then we can pick up your car later."

"You drive and then bring me back. I'm exhausted."

I locked my car and melted into Brett's car. The seat gave me a hug like an old friend. I sighed.

Brett glanced quizzically at me.

"I like these seats," I explained. "They hug like you were meant to sit here."

"That seat was always meant for you," he said.

I really didn't know what to make out of that statement, so I left it alone. But it left me with a warm feeling.

"Jocelyn won't be there," I said as he drove to the office.

"It wouldn't matter either way because she'll be at Longhorn's tonight."

"Does she go there often?"

"She's a regular."

"She told me to have you work every event."

"I'm following you. Where you go, I go."

Brett pulled up alongside the office door. The office was dark. I grabbed my keys out of my purse. Brett hopped out of the car and followed me inside. It only took me a moment to find the lockets while avoiding looking at the bullet holes that littered the wall. I grabbed the box and we left, locking the door behind us. I didn't want to stay there any longer than I had to.

Brett drove back to the conference center.

"I was just going to go home now," I told Brett. "I can work on the lockets there."

"You have a couple of hours and then we need to head to Longhorn's."

I nodded. It was enough time for a shower and to finish a handful of lockets.

"What was that thing Jesse gave you?" I asked Brett.

"I'll show it to you when we get home."

"Why can't you just tell me?"

"Ordinarily, I'd tell you, but I want to see if you can spot Fenwig in it."

"In it? In what?"

Brett didn't say anything.

"Oh, God. It's a sex video, isn't it?"

Brett's lips curved slightly.

"I don't want to watch it."

"You don't have to watch the whole thing. Just watch one part and tell me if you see what I see."

I groaned.

Brett's expression changed. He looked mad.

"Fine, I'll watch the stupid thing," I said to make him happy.

"It's not that. It's your car."

Chapter 11

I turned to look at my car. It was battered by what could only be the result of a sledgehammer. Every window was completely broken out, lights were shattered, the bumper hung by a thread, and every side was riddled with dents.

"My poor car! The Hammer's gone mental!"

"She's been crazy for a long time."

"Who is she? How do you really know it's a she?"

"I still don't know who she is, but I know it's a she. She frequents male strip clubs and targets a dancer. She never gets involved with or hurts the target. She only goes after a woman who gets too close or involved with the target."

"Eve," I said.

Brett nodded. "Eve started dating a stripper in Texas. He was an okay guy, but I could never see what she was doing with him. She started getting threats, and you know the rest."

I sat quietly and held his hand. I'd be scared out of my mind if I was in this alone. Had he known how much danger Eve had been in?

"I tried to protect her, but I didn't know who I was protecting her from," he explained, reading my mind. "She was the Hammer's first victim. I quit my job because they wouldn't let me take the case. They said I was too close to it. I've been following the Hammer, always a step behind until now."

I was at a loss for words.

Brett angled in his seat to look at me. "I'm so sorry I got you involved. I didn't know I had become the target when I met you. It was only after she threatened that I realized it. By then it was too late."

"I'm glad you're the target," I told him, trying for a little bravery on my part. "If it was anyone else, someone would be dead by now."

He kissed the palm of my hand and drove me home.

* * *

Brett made his way into the house first to make sure it was safe.

"I'm going to take a shower," I told him when he returned, adding "alone."

He plopped down on my couch with a wounded expression.

I showered quickly and hurried into my bedroom with a towel wrapped around me, searching for something to wear for tonight. I may as well change into it now since I only had a couple of hours before we had to leave. I searched my drawers and my closet. Both were sparse. I stared and stared into the closet but nothing happened; no outfit jumped out.

Brett knocked on the door and peered in. "You were taking so long I thought I should check."

"You just wanted to see if you could catch me off guard and get a nudie peek."

He smiled. "No harm in a little nudity."

"I'm staring into my closet hoping something will appear for me to wear," I said.

He peeked into my closet. "I know girls keep more clothes than this in their closets. Where's the rest?"

"In the basement next to the washing machine."

"Did you ever think about washing them?"

"Smart ass, of course I've thought about washing them. The machines aren't hooked up. I've been meaning to read the manual, but, hell," I huffed, "I don't want to read the stupid manual."

"I'll pick out an outfit for you," he said.

"No, you won't."

"Don't trust me?"

"Not to dress me."

"What if I hook up your washer and dryer, then can I pick out an outfit?"

I eyed him. "Deal, but don't dress me like a floozy."

"I'll dress you anyway I want to. Besides, I don't have much to choose from."

I perched on my bed while he looked through my clothes. He pulled out low-riding jeans and a scoop-neck T-shirt that was a size or two too small. "Sexy" was scrawled across the chest in bright-pink glitter. I don't know why I'd bought that shirt. I've never even worn it. It just hangs in my closet, occupying a hanger. I prayed my sorry excuse for abs were up to the challenge.

"I'll see you downstairs," Brett said, leaving me to change.

I pulled the shirt on. "Sexy" was stretched to maximum capacity. Cleavage poked out of the scoop neck. I was surprised the glitter wasn't sprinkling off like fairy dust.

I had to jump up and down to pull on the jeans and then lie down on the bed to zip them.

I stood up and looked in the mirror. There was nearly two inches of belly showing. No muffin top or jigglies that I could see; nothing rock hard either. I could get away with the outfit, but I'd have to work harder on other places to draw attention away . . . if that was even possible.

I wrapped my hair in curlers and threw on a robe. I wasn't about to let Brett see the outfit until I had the rest of me in order.

When I stepped off the last stair and into the living room, Brett glanced up to see me in an old fluffy blue robe.

"I'll take it off before we leave and I'm all pretty," I said.

"It'll be worth the wait."

I let myself drop ungracefully to the floor. The jeans wouldn't allow me to bend. Leaning back, I popped o¬pen the top button. Brett raised his eyebrow.

"Don't judge," I said.

The box of lockets sat on the floor next to me. I grabbed the scissors and started cutting out photos, slipping them into the lockets.

"Are you ready for the video?" Brett asked.

"Ugh, no! I'll never be ready for that. But go ahead and get it over with."

Brett opened my laptop and brought out a memory card. He inserted it into the computer and scrolled through the files until he found the right one.

I leaned back and watched Karina and Jesse stumble into a bedroom, groping and kissing each other. It was a slobbery affair, based on the smacks and slurping heard in the audio. Based on the perspective, the camera must have been hidden. Did Jesse even know he was being filmed?

The video showed them kiss, fall to the bed, and then . . . I closed my eyes.

"Open your eyes," Brett said.

"I don't want to see this. They're like animals," I said.

"It's not that bad."

I peeked through my fingers. They were completely naked and very vocal.

"Why did Jesse give this to you?" I asked.

"There," he said, pausing the video. "Do you see in the mirror?"

It was a grainy shot of a man hiding in the closet with a camera.

"Is that . . . Fenwig?"

"I think so," he said and pushed play. "Now watch this."

The man in the closet accidentally made a noise and Jesse heard it. His eyes shot to the closet.

"Jesse, it's nothing. Come back to bed," Karina urged.

Jesse ignored her and leapt from the bed. He threw open the closet door, giving us a very close view of his dingdong.

"Holy moly!" I exclaimed.

Brett shook his head and sighed.

"What the fuck are you doing?" Jesse yelled.

He made a grab for the camera. It was hard to see what was happening after that. A lot of shouting, camera tossing, and then the video ended.

Brett closed the laptop. "I think Fenwig and his wife are into making amateur porn."

"Wouldn't that be bad for Fenwig's career?"

"It could be for their personal collection. Some people get off on it."

"But why kill Jesse?"

"Jesse found out and took the camera. Fenwig would've wanted to shut Jesse up before the police and news got involved. Fenwig had other videos saved on the memory card, too."

"I don't have to watch them, do I?"

"No, you've had enough for one night."

"Why don't you just give him back the memory card?"

"It's my only bargaining chip. If he's the one who killed Jesse, then why should he keep you or me around?"

I nodded. It made sense in a sick sort of way.

"Do you think Jesse would've tried to blackmail Fenwig?"

"Jesse didn't have a very firm grasp on moral codes. I wouldn't put it past him."

I fumbled with another locket. "You were a cop before?"

"Yes, in Houston."

"Cops can't afford Vipers," I told him.

"I'm not a cop anymore."

"Dancers can't afford Vipers," I reworded.

"Some can. Just trust me," he said.

Brett stood, kissed me on the head, and disappeared into the kitchen.

I heard him fumbling through my cupboards and refrigerator. He walked back out with his hands on his hips.

"Do you know you have absolutely nothing to eat here?"

I nodded. "I just got paid. I didn't have any money for food."

"Why didn't you tell me?"

"Tell you what? I just met you, and," I waved my hand, "I go through this all the time before payday. I just think of it as my mandatory diet time. If I actually had money, I wouldn't be able to pry on these jeans."

"Finish getting ready," he said. "We'll eat dinner before Long-horn's."

"I'm not going to dinner in this outfit. That wasn't part of the deal."

Brett picked me up off the floor, placing me on the first step of the stairway. "Go and get dressed in anything you want before both of us starve."

I smiled and ran up the stairs before he could change his mind. I was hungry. I looked in my closet. The problem was this was my last outfit. The rest of the clothes were heavy winter outfits I'd swelter in.

I shed the robe and looked at my tiny T-shirt and jeans. This will have to do. Suck it up and deal with it. It may be fun to pretend I'm something I'm not . . . like Halloween in June.

I used a light touch with most of my makeup, adding a little extra mascara and bright-red lipstick. I unwrapped the curlers from my hair. Big, bouncy curls fell around my shoulders. Arranging the curls without them going limp was a challenge. I had to use a little hair spray, otherwise my curls would be gone within an hour.

Shoes . . . I searched my shoe selection. I may as well finish off the hot-mama look with a pair of four-inch heels. I sat on the bed to slip them onto my feet. I didn't have to stand a lot tonight, so I should be okay.

I stood and looked at the final result. I barely recognized myself. Hopefully, no one else would either.

I carefully walked downstairs in my lethal shoes and stepped into the living room. I posed with my arm on the doorframe and my other hand my hip. I didn't feel sexy but I could at least pretend.

Brett was lounging on the couch, flipping through the television guide. He turned to look at me and dropped the remote. His eyes darkened with a glint of wickedness.

"Come here," he said.

"No, I don't like that look in your eyes. You'll mess me up, and then you won't get dinner because I'll have to start all over."

He rose, taking a few steps toward me. I was closer to his height with my heels. Brett pulled me in, kissing me hard.

"I can't take much more of this, Mars. You're driving me to the brink of insanity." Brett's hands roamed.

"I guess that means you like it," I said, cleaning the lipstick off his lips.

"I do." He kissed me again. "Let's skip dinner. You'll be enough to satisfy any hunger I have and more." He bit my bottom lip playfully. "Plus, I don't want any other guys to look at you."

"I'm hungry," I said, pushing past him. I threw my purse over my shoulder, fixed my lipstick in the mirror by the door, and strutted out.

Mrs. Janowski was rocking in her chair on her porch. A large glass of iced tea was at her side.

"Mars, is that you?" she hollered.

"Yes, it's me," I hollered back.

"Hot damn!" she exclaimed, slapping her thigh. "And here I thought you needed more spunk."

"If she gets any more spunk, I'll need an ambulance," Brett called to Mrs. Janowski.

She chuckled.

"Where are we going?" I asked once we were in the car.

He peered down at my shirt. "Well, I can't take you anywhere respectable."

"There's a bar and grill close to Longhorn's. It looks like a hole in the wall, but I heard the food is good and greasy."

"I've been there," he said. "We'll fit in."

"Of course you've been there."

"What does that mean?"

I arched my eyebrow and he grinned.

The Road Hog Bar catered to big, rugged men with leather jackets and Harleys and their scantily clad women . . . oh great, I'm going to be one of them.

The patrons at the bar turned in their seats to size us up when we entered. I was about ready to turn and run, but Brett kept a firm grip and steered me in. One by one the tattooed men turned away.

I surveyed the women. Most of them were pretty, but they had a look to them. Like too much time spent in the dingy bar and not enough time in fresh air. One of them was sitting on a man's lap at the bar. I couldn't see the man's face, but he had nice arms that, oddly, weren't tattooed.

"Brett, grab us a table, and I'll go get drinks," I said.

He caught my arm before I left for the bar. "You may as well order food for us too," he said, pushing money into my hand. "There isn't much customer service here."

"I can pay."

"How?"

I didn't think about that. My money was in the bank and we didn't stop at the ATM. I doubted this place took anything except cash.

I took the money in defeat and wedged in between the man with nice arms and a hairy man with a bandana wrapped around his head. The aging bartender acknowledged me with a nod and a finger that said one minute.

I waited. The music was old hair-band rock. Axel Rose was bellowing "Welcome to the Jungle," and I surmised I may have actually landed in a tattoo jungle. The music was loud, but not loud enough to drown out the conversation to my left.

The woman laughed and said, "Do you really have a Harley?"

I couldn't hear what the man said, but it must have been a dirty suggestion. She laughed again and said, "You're a naughty boy. I want to give you a test drive."

My eyes searched for the bartender; I really didn't want to hear this. The bartender must have gone in back. I glanced over at Brett and shrugged. He didn't seem to mind, giving me the impression that he was staring at my rear end this entire time.

The bartender reappeared and took down my order. I was interrupted when the woman tried to slide off of the man's lap and stumbled into me.

"Oh, sorry," she said, righting herself by hanging onto me. "I just need to go to the restroom. I must've had a little too much to drink."

"No problem," I said, letting her through.

She turned to the man. "I'll be right back, babycakes."

I turned to the bartender and finished my order. The bartender took my cash and walked to the register. I stood, waiting for the change. Out of the corner of my eye, I could see the man with the nice arms was studying me. I pretended to ignore him.

"What's your name?" the man asked.

"None of your business," I said as I turned to him.

It was Evan. My mouth dropped open. He took a good, long look at me. The realization hit him and his eyes widened.

"Holy shit! Mars, is that you?" His eyes roamed, taking in all of me. "I've never seen you like this. You're always beautiful, but this look could make me beg. Come home with me," he urged with his playboy smile.

"I'm here with Brett."

His eyes drifted through the bar until he spotted Brett at the table. "The hell you are," he said. "Only one thing can happen when a girl dresses this way."

"Oh yeah? And what's that, babycakes?" I asked.

"You aren't going to find out with him," he stated. "You're coming with me."

"What about the girl who was just sitting on your lap?"

"She doesn't mean anything to me."

"They never mean anything to you," I said, picking up the change minus a few dollars for the bartender. "I don't want to be someone who doesn't mean anything."

His arctic blue eyes sent frost into mine. He was upset to find me with another man. I wasn't too happy to find him with another woman, but I'm used to it. He always has women trailing after him. They'd run over tacks to be with him. I wasn't one of them. I'd never be one of them.

I turned to leave. He gently held my wrist. "I'm sorry, sugar," he said, letting go.

I didn't look at him but walked to the table and sat down by Brett. His jaw was rigid.

I smiled at him, brushing his stubble with the back of my hand, "Don't worry about it," I murmured, more for myself than him.

Brett relaxed and held my hand. Moments later, Evan and the woman left the bar. He shot a final look at me before he left. My heart hiccupped as he left with her. I heard a motorcycle take off. Gone again.

When our food was dropped on the table, Brett pulled me onto his lap.

"How are you going to eat if I'm sitting on you?" I asked.

"You can feed me."

"I'm not going to feed you."

"Then I'll pass out on the dance floor from starvation, and you'll have to pull the women off me."

I rolled my eyes. How was I going to feed him a greasy hamburger and not get us both stained? I cut a small piece off, placing it in his mouth. His teeth grazed against my fingers, licking my fingertips.

"Do that again and I'll let the women ravage you."

He chuckled. "You're not playing fair."

"When have you ever played fair?"

"Never."

I fed him most of the burger and fries before he freed me and leaned back to watch me.

"I never get tired of looking at you," he said.

"You've only known me for five days."

"Mmm, and it's been a very unsatisfying five days."

I relaxed in my chair, licking the grease off my fingers one by one. He groaned.

* * *

We entered through the back door of Longhorn's since the front door was still locked. Some of the dancers were already there and looked over when Brett and I appeared. He gave them a dark look that could only mean "back off, she's mine."

"I can't let you back in the dressing room for obvious reasons. Head to the front and wait there." He shoved money into my front pocket. "You'll be safe at the bar with Annie. Many of the dancers don't go by the bar."

I nodded and turned to leave.

"Mars, I understand why you don't want to be here," Brett said. "If our lives were reversed, I couldn't bear to see you up on stage."

I gave him a small smile and made my way to the front. Annie was there getting ready for the night.

"Hi, Annie," I said, hopping onto a barstool.

She looked at me funny.

"It's Mars."

"Mars?" She blinked. "I didn't recognize you."

"I know. It's a bit much." I gestured to myself. "I'm having some fun with it."

"I've seen some pretty trashy people walk through these doors, but you don't look trashy. More va-va-va-voom," she said with a laugh. "Are you here with Brett?"

"Yes," I said. "He told me I'd be safe at the bar."

"Most likely, yes. The dancers stay away from the bar and try to work the rest of the room. Every once in a while they come over to harass anyone who looks like they're trying to hide."

"I'll remember that," I said, inspecting myself in a compact. "Keeping this face and hair intact is a lot of work."

"Brett's worth it though, right?" she asked.

"He is worth it. I'm only doing this for the night, and then I'm going back to being me," I said, snapping the compact closed.

Annie stepped to the front door to unlock it. She reached up in the window and pulled the chain to light up the open sign.

"Do you ever date any of the dancers?" I asked Annie.

"I have before, but I don't now," she said. "It's too hard of a life. To watch them dance and have women fawn over them. It doesn't stop at the stage, you know? They give off a vibe or aura that women can't stay away from. It always ended badly, so I've given them up for good."

"I'm not sure how it will end with Brett, but I'm going to enjoy it while it lasts," I said.

"I have to turn on the music until the DJ arrives," Annie said. "Can you tell the guys we'll be ready in five minutes?"

"But there isn't anyone here."

"There will be any moment now."

I remembered what Brett had said about the men, and I didn't want to go back there. I pulled out my cell phone to relay the message from the safety of my seat. There was a text from Evan. I hesitated before opening it.

It's true. They don't mean anything to me, but you will always mean EVERYTHING to me. Don't give up on me before you give me a chance.

I sensed heat on my back. Brett. I peered up at him. His hard expression told me he had read the text. I tucked the phone into my pocket.

"I was going to call you. Annie said you should be ready in five minutes. I didn't want to go backstage."

Brett nodded. He was dressed in a construction outfit this time. His jeans were tight. I traced the lines on his oiled abs with my finger and he gave a small shudder. I smiled.

"Careful," he warned. "I can't go on stage if I'm worked up. I'll have to find someone to help alleviate the situation."

"Who, me?" A sly smile escaped.

"No one else but you, sweet thing," he said, kissing my neck. "Can you help me? I can't fasten the bottom of the jeans. They're so tight, I bust out every time I bend."

"Couldn't one of the guys in back help you?"

"Yes, but I like it better when you touch me."

I knelt down and sealed the pant legs. On my way back up, I took the scenic route, catching a glimpse of some spectacular sights.

"I saw that," he said.

"I'm just admiring the view."

"I want to kiss you, but that damn red lipstick keeps standing in my way."

"Good to know," I said. "You better go backstage before ladies start showing up."

He brushed his fingers against my cheek and turned to leave.

Within a minute after he left, women trickled in. They were mostly in groups, some bachelorette parties, but every once in a while a lady flying solo showed up. Could the Hammer be one of these ladies? I observed each one from my seat. They all seemed normal to me.

"Let me get you something to drink before it becomes a madhouse in here," Annie offered.

"That sounds great."

She mixed me a brilliant blue concoction. I tasted it.

"Kool-Aid?"

"Blue Zombie," she said. "Sip it or it'll kick your ass."

"Thanks," I said.

With my drink in my hand, I settled and watched women fill in around the catwalk. In a matter of seconds, the atmosphere was about to change. How do men do that? They have the unique ability to throw life into a topsy-turvy roller coaster. I guess they could say the same about women.

The women here looked normal, average. Not knowing what the Hammer looked like made the job of finding her nearly impossible. Like finding my Uncle Auggie's Viagra bottle the time his dog stole it and ran halfway across town with it. He never did find it, but the dog returned home with disturbing side effects. Unless the Hammer made a move, I didn't have a chance of finding her.

"Annie, have you ever heard of the Hammer before?" I asked as she poured drinks.

"Is that a rock band or something?"

"No, it's a serial killer. A woman who's killed other women who have become involved with a male exotic dancer she's stalking."

"You're putting me on. I've never heard of such a thing."

"No, I'm serious. She has her eye on Brett, and I've been threatened. She beat the hell out of my car with a sledgehammer and broke into my house."

"Sounds like you need to be careful."

"I can't imagine who it could be. No one here looks like they could be a serial killer. Brett and I aren't even serious."

"Have you been seen together?" Annie asked. "Like on a date?"

"Yes."

"I would assume anyone might take that as a relationship. Or at least the start of one."

"I guess you have a point."

"Maybe you should give him up. Is he worth your life?"

The DJ pumped the music. I quickly peeked to see who was on-stage. No Brett. I breathed a sigh of relief. I turned to my drink, keeping my back turned to the dancers.

Brett was right. So far, none of the dancers came to the bar.

I should have brought the rest of the lockets to work on. Sitting here with no one to talk to was going to be very boring. I could take a peek at the dancers . . . no, not worth it.

I slipped out my phone. I never replied to Evan's text. I didn't even have a clue how to respond to it. How can I give up on him when he never gave himself the chance to be in a relationship?

The music changed. My heart palpitated. I snuck a quick peek. Brett was on stage. Damn, he was hot with the lights glittering against his vast, rippling muscles. His presence eclipsed the rest of the dancers. My eyes glazed in a trance that could only see him. As the music peaked, he tore off his vest and swung it in the air. I coughed, sputtering my drink.

Did he just bite a dollar out of a woman's cleavage?

Squelching a jealous urge to stuff the dollar back where it came from, I refocused on my drink. It was only a matter seconds before my eyes returned.

If I was the Hammer, Brett would be my objective too.

Damn him! I'm all flustered again.

Brett locked eyes on me. His hand moved tantalizingly slow to his jeans. Women screamed for him to take it off, and I watched with drool forming at the corners of my mouth. The beat of the music hit; he ripped them off in one fluid motion. I jumped, sloshing my drink over the rim of the glass. He smirked.

I quickly turned back to the bar, but I could still see him in the reflection of the mirror behind the bar. It was like watching through a blurry television.

A woman sat next to me. She was pretty with dark hair and eyes. She had an air of strength to her. She looked familiar to me.

"Hey, Annie," the woman yelled over the music. "Give me a beer."

Annie nodded and brought her a beer, charging it to her account. The woman took a long swig from the bottle and settled into her seat.

"Hey, hon," she greeted me with a hint of a Southern accent. "Who's your man?"

"The construction worker," I answered. "How did you know?"

"Hon, if you're sitting at the bar not watching them, then you're here with one of them."

"You look familiar to me. Have we met before?"

The woman gave me a glance and shook her head. "I don't think we've met. But I come in here all the time." She pointed to the stage. "Tarzan is mine. I come here to fend off the women."

I looked over to see Tarzan. He had perfect cocoa skin and a nicely sculpted body.

"I must have seen you last week then. I was here for a bachelorette party. Your Tarzan is good-looking," I said.

She nodded. She's probably heard that a lot.

"I'm Renee," she introduced herself.

"Nice to meet you. I'm Mars."

"You're Mars?" she asked.

"Yeah, do you know me?"

"No, but it's starting to make sense now."

"What makes sense?"

"Last night, one of your man's fans had a fit because he wasn't here."

"He was scheduled to work last night?"

"Yeah. You didn't know?" Renee eyed me. I'm sure she knew exactly what was up in Tarzan's life. Hell, she probably kept his calendar for him.

"No, I just started seeing him."

"Well, you'll learn to keep better track of your man. These men tend to have a roaming eye, and where their eyes go, so does their penis."

I sputtered on my drink again. Through my coughs, I nodded for her to continue.

"Anyway, she found out that he was with Mars. I didn't know who Mars was. I thought it may have been a stage name. Sorry, but that's a strange name you've got there."

Renee looked me over. "But now that I've met you, I think you can pull it off. Not many people named Mars would be able to."

"I've had thirty years of practice fitting into the name."

"No, you didn't fit into it. It fits you."

I smiled, taking a sip of my blue juice. It was starting to make me sparkly . . . yes, sparkly and queasy.

"You'll want to be careful with that drink," Renee cautioned. "One of those could knock out an elephant."

"It's already started. I can't feel my toes." I yanked off my heels. "Of course, it could be these shoes."

Renee inspected me. "How many fingers am I holding up?"

"Two."

"Okay, you're fine. You may want to switch to something else."

"You're probably right."

"Annie," I called to her from across the bar. "Can you get me something fruity and light on alcohol?"

Annie started mixing a drink but had to go to the back to grab some more juice.

Renee watched Tarzan intently, making sure no woman got too handsy.

Annie came back with the juice and finished my drink. She handed me a mai tai. I took a small sip.

The mirror reflected Brett leaving the stage. I sighed and stirred my drink.

"Renee, who was the woman who got upset yesterday?"

"I don't know her name, but she's a regular." Renee looked around the room. "I don't see her here. After her outburst yesterday, she may not come back."

A woman stood to the side of me. "Excuse me," she called to Annie.

Annie walked over to the woman. I looked at her reflection in the mirror. It was Karina Fenwig.

"Can you give this to the construction worker?"

"Haven't you had enough?" Annie muttered.

Karina glared at Annie. "Don't start with me. I'm cleaning up enough messes without your crap."

"Be careful," Annie warned.

"Is that a threat or concern?" Karina sneered, tilting her head back to let out a callous laugh. "Never mind, I know exactly what it is. Just do this for me. I won't bother you again."

Annie nodded, tucking the envelope behind the bar. Karina took a last look at the dancers before she strutted out. On her way out, she gave a tight nod to Renee. Renee returned the nod.

"What was that about?" I asked Renee.

"I always like to say keep your friends close and your enemies closer, but I can't even follow my own advice with her. You better watch yourself. It seems like you have competition," Renee said.

"Is that what it is?"

"Competition isn't so bad. It keeps you on your toes. But there are some people here you don't want to compete against."

"Even my boss is after him," I confided. "I'm not even sure what he sees in me to keep him interested. How do I compete with all these women?"

"Hon, have you looked at yourself in the mirror? You could get any man here." She paused, wagging her finger at me. "Just don't be messing with mine."

"Promise," I said and crossed my heart. "I have enough men problems."

After a few songs, the mai tai was gone. I was ready to order another one, but my mind was fuzzy and it was spreading to my limbs.

"Renee, can you have Annie get me some water? She was heavy-handed with the alcohol. I'm not feeling too good right now."

Renee cruised over to Annie at the other side of the bar. She came back with black coffee and set it in front of me.

"Here you go. This might make you feel better," Renee said.

I took a sip and the warm liquid hit my stomach. It wasn't smooth or soothing.

"Girl, you're turning green."

"I feel horrible."

"Let's go backstage and you can lie down."

"Brett said not to go back there because of the men."

"They don't mess with me."

I stood slowly, pausing so the room would tilt back to normal. Renee grabbed me and my purse, and we wound our way to the back.

A woman at a table met me with hard, narrow eyes. Her head was covered with tight, frizzy curls.

"Mars?" she asked.

I nodded.

"Payback's a bitch," she snarled. "Stay away from him or next time my hand will slip a little bit more."

Renee whispered into my ear, "That's her."

"What did you do?" I panicked.

She cackled, making her eyes bug out.

"Renee, get me backstage quickly."

Renee pushed through the crowd of women until we made it backstage. Brett spotted us from the stage and ran back to meet us.

"What the hell happened?" he asked.

I laughed hysterically. It came out of nowhere. How could I not laugh? Brett was morphing into a bumble bee, and Renee into a bright yellow flower.

"Buzz," I mimicked a bee, poking him in the stomach.

"I think she's been drugged," the yellow flower said. "There's a freaky lady out there."

"A talking flower," I gasped.

The room grew dark and heavy. My body sank to the floor, twitching. Giant, hairy spiders crawled on me. They nested into my hair.

"Get them off!" I shrieked. "Get them off!"

Chapter 12

My eyes opened to an unfamiliar room. Lead must have replaced my brain, because I couldn't lift my head. I blinked, letting my eyes adjust to the brightness. I squeezed them tight. The piercing light was too bright.

My head pounded like someone had taken a sledgehammer to it. My heart stopped. Sledgehammer? I reached my hand up to inspect my head. I clenched my eyes, searching for damage. I didn't feel anything out of the ordinary, just the big knot I've had since I flew off the swing when I was six. My dad had said I could be anyone I wanted to be as long as I put my mind to it. I put my mind to becoming Superman . . . it didn't work.

I let out a sigh of relief that my head was still intact. Maybe if I go back to sleep, I'll wake up in my own room. Dreamland was about to swallow me when I heard footsteps. A light kiss fell upon my forehead.

"Wake up, sleeping beauty." A smooth voice drifted to a happy part of my brain that wasn't filled with muck.

"My head hurts," I murmured, squeezing my eyes closed even tighter.

"You were heavily drugged."

"She had crazy eyes and bad hair," I said, trying to remember.

I cracked my eyes open to see a fuzzy outline. I didn't have to open them more to know who it was. Judging from the velvety voice, it was Evan.

"Why are you here?" I asked, squinting at the light.

"Why do you think? You scared the hell out of me, Mars. You were overdosing. I almost lost you in the ambulance." He smoothed my hair and placed a light kiss on my lips. "Don't ever do that to me again."

I tried to sit.

"Relax," he ordered. "Your body has gone through trauma."

"When can I leave?"

"Later."

"I have things to do."

"You can't even sit on your own."

"The rehearsal dinner for Kym's wedding is tonight. I have the Stevenson party too. Oh, and I need to pick up my dress." A list percolated through the sludge.

He poured some water for me to drink. "You're infuriating."

"I'm not."

"Did you get my message?"

"Yes."

"You didn't reply."

"I was drugged."

"I'm here now. What's your reply?"

"You should be nice to sick people. You know, give them a break."

"Sugar, I've been far too nice to you. If I had any brains, I'd have seduced you years ago."

"Nice try. You said I shouldn't give up on you."

"Yes."

"You gave up on relationships, therefore me, long before."

He was silent for a moment. Evan brushed the hair from my face. His fingers lingered lightly on my cheek. "I didn't do anything with the girl from the bar," he said. "I dropped her off at her apartment and drove home." He looked as if he were grasping for an explanation. "It didn't feel right. It hasn't for a long time."

I gave him a small smile, slipping my hand into his. I meant for it to soothe him, but I felt warm and cozy too. "When did you buy a Harley?"

"You were drugged to an inch of your life, and you're asking about my Harley?"

I nodded. Harleys were born and bred in Wisconsin. Call me a schmuck, but a gorgeous man with a Harley between his legs was better than cheesecake . . . unless it's turtle cheesecake.

I even squeaked by the road test and got my motorcycle license. I prefer to sit behind a man and wrap my arms around him instead of riding by myself. Not that I've had much experience either way. Plus, I can't afford a motorcycle and, frankly, I scare myself when I drive one.

Cheesecake is far safer.

"I bought it a month ago. I'll take you on a ride soon."

"Can I drive?"

"No."

A figure appeared in the doorframe behind Evan. Evan glanced behind him, setting his face hard. He gave me a kiss on the forehead, allowing his hair to fall gently on my face. He didn't linger long.

"I'll see you later, sugar."

Evan turned, giving a tight nod to Brett. Brett returned the nod and walked in. He stood by my bed, reaching for my hand.

"You look like hell," I told him.

His face was drawn and white. Deep lines appeared where there had been none before. His weight pressed down on him.

"I don't want to talk about me; I want to talk about you. How are you feeling?"

"My head hurts, my body hurts, and even my baby toe hurts."

Brett pulled a chair next to me, collapsing into it. He threaded his fingers through mine.

"The woman who drugged you has been booked. You'll eventually need to talk to the police so they can finish their report."

"Is she the Hammer?"

Brett shook his head. "No. I've been looking through her file and she's been in jail during two of the murders. It doesn't add up that she would try to hurt you. This isn't in her rap sheet that landed her in jail before."

"Renee told me that she was mad that you weren't at Longhorn's the other night and that she made a scene."

"That's news to me. No one told me about it. What I did find out was that someone wired a lot of money into her account. I have a feeling she was paid to drug you."

"Can the wire transfer be traced?"

"It led to a dead end."

"I don't understand. Why are people coming out of the woodwork to harm me? People used to like me," I said. "I've never even been in a fight. I've never had a black eye. Why now?"

"I'm so sorry," he said. His shoulders slumped over slightly and his grip tightened on my hand.

"Ow," I whimpered.

"What?" Brett bolted out of the chair. "What's wrong?"

"You hurt my hand."

Brett fell back in the chair. "I'm so fucking sorry," he said, barely audible.

He was taking this hard. This was personal to him. I'm sure he had gone through this with his sister and now it's happening all over again.

"You haven't slept, have you?"

Brett shook his head.

"Please, go get some sleep," I said. "I'm fine. The woman is in custody, and I have things to do today. I can't have a sleepy shadow."

A sliver of a smile formed. "The doctors said you can't leave until they've done more tests on you."

"You go to sleep, and I'll harass the doctors to get me released."

"I'm sleeping here," he insisted.

"Sleep wherever you want."

"Scoot over and let me in." He winked.

"I can barely fit in the bed myself."

Brett stood to give me a kiss. "Goodnight."

"Goodnight."

He sank back into the chair and leaned his head back to rest against the wall. He was out within a couple of minutes. I pushed the nurse's call button.

A stout pixie with fire-engine-red hair came fluttering into my room. "You're awake." She inspected my eyes and smiled. "How do you feel?"

"I hurt, but I'm okay."

"That was a really nasty overdose," she said. "The lab is still trying to figure out the concoction. It's amazing you're here with us."

"That's what I've been told." I looked at Brett. The nurse followed my gaze.

"He and Evan brought you in last night. They waited the whole night. The two of them looked like lions stalking their territory. He," the nurse pointed at Brett, "was on the phone making tons of phone calls that didn't look pleasant. There were men who kept coming in and out talking to him. One of them was really scary. He had a tarantula tattoo on his neck. I was about ready to get security involved."

"You're sure about the tattoo?"

"Oh yes, I couldn't miss something like that."

I glanced over at Brett. He was still sleeping. Who is this guy? Why was he talking to the scary tattoo guy?

"When can I leave?" I asked.

"The doctor wants to do some more blood work before you can be released. We want to make sure you're all back to normal."

"Can they be done now? I have things to do."

"I'll see what I can do, but you're on hospital time now. We have our own speed," she said with a chuckle.

"Anything you can do to speed up the process would make me very happy."

"Just rest some more. Breakfast will be arriving soon."

I nodded and leaned back. What the hell is going on? I narrowed in on Brett. He's keeping something from me. Is he working with the bad guys? Is he one of them, and I've fallen for his charm and unbelievably good looks? I hoped I wasn't such a sucker. But looking at him makes me forget all common sense.

I really didn't know anything about him. He may not even be Brett Thompson. His driver's license could be fake. But why meet my parents and clean my house? He had my car painted too. I softened. He told me to trust him. I'll have to trust him until I can figure out more.

I searched for my phone. My purse and clothes were nowhere in sight. The hospital phone was across the room. I wasn't confident enough to trek over there with an IV stuck in my arm. This sucks!

I looked at Brett. He must have a phone on him. He's not wearing a jacket, so it must be in his pants pocket. A sliver of a shiny black object poked out of his front pocket. If I stretched, I might be able to just reach it. My twitchy finger got the best of me. I reached my hand to his pocket. My fingers tightened on the edge of the phone. I held on firmly as I slid it from his pocket. He moved a little, allowing the phone to glide into my hand.

His phone was sleek and new. I touched the screen and the phone came to life. A woman stared back at me from the screen. She had the same eyes as Brett . . . Eve.

Would it be invading his privacy if I looked at the other pictures on his phone? Probably, I sighed. However, he could be a bad guy, and then it wouldn't be invading his privacy, just investigating to protect myself, I reasoned.

A message popped on the screen and beeped. I jumped from surprise, nearly dropping the phone. I read the message. It's not my fault. I'm drugged.

Meet me at 11:00 tonight.

Uh-oh, I really didn't want to read that. I quickly slipped the phone back into Brett's pocket, breathing a sigh of relief when he didn't move. I wasn't meant to be James Bond . . . or even Money Penny.

I called for the nurse again, and she dug out my phone for me. I should have thought of that to begin with. I dialed Emmy.

"Emmy, I need a favor."

"Oh, sure," Emmy said.

"Can you go to my house and get the lockets? I couldn't finish them."

"Oh," she said wryly. "You and Brett must have had some night."

"Yes, but it's not what you think. I'm in the hospital."

"Why? What happened?"

"A lot, but I don't want to get into it right now."

"Okay, but you'll tell me later, right?"

"Yes. You'll need to come here and get the key."

"I'll come over now since Jocelyn isn't here. Curtis can watch the phone for me."

"Can I ask one more favor?"

"Anything."

"Can you pick up my bridesmaid dress?"

"Sure, no problem."

My breakfast arrived after I hung up with Emmy.

It was dismal.

I pushed it away and left it for dead, which, judging from its appearance, happened years ago.

"Hey, girl," Renee said as she appeared in the doorway. "Good to see you alive and well. You had everyone scared." She looked over at Brett sleeping and chuckled. "You should've seen him. As soon as you fell to the ground twitching, he told me to call nine-one-one. He bounded off the stage, diving on the woman who drugged you. It was complete chaos. She was flat on the ground, and he handcuffed her to the pole until the police came. I don't know where he got the handcuffs. He could've had them tucked in his thong." She smirked. "Make sure to ask him, won't you?"

I smiled.

"Then the ambulance showed up," Renee continued, "and there was this drop-dead gorgeous EMT giving you mouth-to-mouth because you stopped breathing. I'm telling you, girl, I wouldn't mind getting drugged if that EMT was going to give me mouth-to-mouth."

"Evan," I said. He gave me mouth-to-mouth? I touched my lips in wonder.

"You know him?"

I nodded.

"That explains why he and Brett were looking like two alpha dogs trying to get the same bone."

I groaned.

"Yeah, tell me about it. They both rode in the back of the ambulance. I thought for sure you'd never make it to the hospital. I had to follow them because Brett was still wearing his thong."

I smiled at the picture forming in my head.

"Yeah, it was good," she agreed.

Renee looked at my breakfast. "This is what they gave you to eat?"

"Yes."

"Oh, hell no!" she barked.

Brett stirred but didn't wake.

"These Northern hospitals don't know squat about food. They should serve you biscuits and gravy. Maybe a little fried chicken and sweet potato pie."

I eyed Renee. "They wouldn't serve that to sick patients, would they?"

"I don't know. I've never been sick. But I'd rather starve than eat what they served you." Renee whipped out her phone. "Sweet cheeks, pick up a giant breakfast for Mars. They're trying to starve her after she almost died. Damn hospital is probably going to charge her a hundred dollars for this junk."

I cringed. I didn't even want to guess how much this was going to cost me. All health care for Jocelyn McCain Events was pumped into Jocelyn's plastic surgeon's pocket.

Renee hung up the phone. "Don't you worry about a thing."

The door to the room crashed open and in stormed my mom like someone stole her last bottle of wine. "My baby!" she cried.

Brett woke up for her entrance. Seeing that it was my mother, he fell back asleep. Great. This is the time I could use reinforcement, and he falls back asleep.

Renee gawked at her in awe; a woman after her own heart.

"Mom, calm down. I'm okay."

"You're not okay! You're a druggie!"

"Mom, there's a difference between being a druggie and getting drugged."

"Well, which one are you? I woke up to find a voicemail from Brett saying that you were at the hospital for an overdose. Is he the dealer?" She pointed to Brett. "He seemed like such a nice young man."

"Mom, a lunatic woman—who you are starting to resemble—drugged me. Brett and Renee saved me."

Mom turned to Renee. Renee inched back, a little worried.

"Come here," Mom demanded, a catch in her voice.

Renee crept up. My mother grabbed her, crushing her in a hug. Renee snapped her head toward me. Her eyes bugged out. I shrugged. She was on her own.

My dad entered the room. "How are you feeling, honey?" He gave me a kiss on the forehead. "You gave everyone a scare."

"I didn't like it too much either."

My dad sighed at the sight of my mom squeezing Renee. He attempted to pry Renee loose from Mom's python death grip.

"Diane, please don't squeeze her so much. We don't need another injury."

Diane nodded and let go.

Renee sucked in air and clutched her chest. "I thought I was a goner."

Sweet cheeks arrived with breakfast. It smelled greasy. Heaven! He did his best to squeeze in next to my bed. "Here you go. One giant breakfast with all the naughty, greasy stuff you could possibly eat."

I smiled and thanked him. I could see why Renee liked him; he really was a sweet cheeks.

The door opened again, but I couldn't see who it was. The room was filled to capacity.

"Mars?" Kym's head popped up next to my bed. Sweet cheeks gave a small start at her unexpected appearance.

"Mars, what happened? Are you okay?"

"I'll be fine."

She sighed. "Not to sound uncaring, but will you still make it to the wedding?"

"Of course," I reassured her. "I wouldn't miss it."

"What about dinner tonight? You don't have to come if you're not feeling good."

"I'm trying to get the doctors to release me as soon as possible."

Kym bounced and gave me a kiss on the cheek.

The door opened yet again. I expected the room to burst at the seams at any moment. I didn't have a clue how Brett could sleep through this.

"Mars?"

"I'm over here, Emmy."

Emmy made her way through. She only stepped on one toe. "Sorry!" she called back.

"Emmy, my key is in my purse, but I don't know where it is. Hang on." I pressed the nurse's call button. "The nurse can find it for me. Are you and Curtis going to be okay for the event tonight?"

"Yes, we'll be fine. Don't worry."

"I'll try to stop by. I know it's going to be beautiful."

I couldn't see the pixie nurse, but I heard her stern voice scold, "What is going on in here?"

A dazed Brett jumped to his feet. He knocked my mom into my dad but caught their arms before they tumbled over.

"Everyone needs to leave," the nurse belted. She pushed Brett back into his seat. "Not you. You need more sleep, and I don't mind looking at you."

"Wait," I said before anyone could leave the room. "I need to give Emmy the key to my house."

"Here, take this one," Brett said, slipping my key off his key ring.

Everyone in the room raised an eyebrow. They cast a quizzical gaze at Brett and then at me.

"It was in the rock," I explained.

Everyone nodded their heads like they completely understood my fake rock problem.

My head sank back into the pillow. I need a new rock. My eyes were heavy. I could barely keep them open. Maybe just a little more sleep.

I sat straight up. Brett was in the chair next to me. His face was hard and his eyes glared.

"What time is it?" I asked.

"Ten to four."

"How do you know it's ten to four? You didn't even look at your watch."

"I've been looking at it every minute for the past four hours."

"Are you waiting for something?"

"Yes."

He was being difficult. I couldn't get a read on him. Perhaps sleeping in a chair wasn't the best idea.

"Do you mind telling me what you are waiting for?"

"Four o'clock."

This was becoming tedious.

"Damn it!" I growled. "Just tell me what's going on, or I'm checking myself out. I have two dinners that need me, and I'm starving. I need food and I need it now!"

Brett's expression didn't change. "At four o'clock, you can be discharged from the hospital," he explained, but his jaw remained rigid. "At four o'clock, I'm getting you the hell out of here."

"Good. I have things to do, and I need to change."

"That's not what I meant. I'm taking you out of the state and putting you into hiding until I find the Hammer."

"No."

"No?"

"You heard me."

"I heard you, but it's not going to change anything."

"Brett, if that's your name, I'm not going anywhere except to the two dinners tonight and then to the wedding tomorrow. If you take me anywhere else, it'll be kidnapping. I hear that the police frown upon that. And if you really were a cop, you wouldn't try it."

Brett's brow darkened. "You know damn well what my name is."

"No, I don't. I saw your license, but it could be fake."

"It's not fake. I thought we were past this. I thought you trusted me."

"I do," I said, and then corrected myself. "I did until I heard the tarantula goon was here to talk to you."

"I talked to him."

"Obviously. So, what am I supposed to think about that?"

Brett didn't say anything.

"Who are you supposed to meet at eleven tonight?"

His eyes widened in surprise. His jaw clenched. I really hope he's not the bad guy. He could scare the begeebers out of anyone, including me. Brett stood, moving closer. I jumped out of bed, holding my gown shut. He was quick, cornering me before I could run away.

He pulled me into him, lifting my chin so that our eyes met. "What else do you know?"

"Nothing," I hedged. I wanted to tell him that I knew all his secrets, but I couldn't lie to him. He had a power over me that I couldn't explain or understand. "I pulled out your phone to call Emmy and ask her to pick up the lockets. The message came in before I could call. I panicked and put the phone back in your pocket."

"You picked my pocket while I was sleeping?"

"It was for a good cause, and I put it back."

He cracked a smile and gave a small laugh. "I'll have to remember to keep my pockets away from you."

His fingers pulled the strings on my gown, untying them. His hands slipped into the opening, making the gown fall to the floor. He pressed me into him.

"You feel amazing," he groaned before scooting me into the bathroom. "Emmy brought clothes and bath things for you." He took one last lingering look before closing the door.

I grabbed the bag sitting on the floor and looked inside. She had brought my little black dress, heels, sandals, and everything from my bathroom, excluding the bathroom sink.

I took a hot, steamy shower, letting the water beat down on my shoulders. Brett passed through my mind. I may be a fool, but I trust him.

An image flashed. Brett in the shower, wet with soap bubbles sliding down his chest, gave me a jolt below the belt. I turned the shower knob to cold. Get out of my head, Brett. I shrieked as the icy-cold water hit me.

Brett barged in, throwing open the curtain. "What's wrong?"

"Cold." I shivered.

He sighed and turned the knob to warm. He took a good long look at me . . . wet, soapy, and frozen-hard nipples.

He groaned and slid the curtain shut.

I wasn't about to tell him that an image of him was the result of him seeing the exact same image of me.

I toweled off and fumbled through the bag for underwear.

"Oh, no!"

"I'm not coming in this time," Brett said outside the door.

Emmy didn't pack any underwear. I sighed. I didn't need a bra. The dress was backless and the front was low-cut and form-fitted to hold up the girls. The panties could be a problem, though. The skirt of the dress had a fun, swishy flow. It hung about an inch or two above my knees. The only problem: one gust of wind and I'm flashing the world like Marilyn Monroe. Good thing Madison isn't big enough to have subways or their subsequent air vents.

I chose the sandals for now. I'd break out the heels later. I did a quick twist with my hair and clipped it up. I packed up the remaining items scattered in the bathroom and walked out to find Brett smiling. His bad mood had disintegrated.

I dropped the bag on the floor and pushed the call button for the nurse.

"Can I go now?" I asked when she appeared.

"Yes, I'll get the wheelchair for you."

"I'm not going in a wheelchair. I'm perfectly fine."

"I know you are, but we have a policy."

I tapped my foot impatiently.

Brett smirked.

* * *

"We need to go home," I said as Brett drove out of the hospital parking lot.

I heard the snap of handcuffs and felt cold metal enclose around my wrist.

"What the hell?"

"You gave me no choice," Brett said simply. He snapped the other cuff on his wrist. "I'm officially kidnapping you."

Chapter 13

I glowered at Brett as I pulled at the handcuff around my wrist, hoping it'd magically fall off.

"We're stuck together until I get you to a safe place," Brett said.

"I told you before; I'm going to the dinners tonight. I can't walk out on Kym."

"I already told her that you can't make it tonight."

My blood spit fire. "You had no right to do that," I barked.

"You're right, I didn't. But I'm trying to protect you from a serial killer."

I stewed.

"What if we stay handcuffed and you take me to the dinners?" I negotiated.

"No, I can't protect you when your movements are being watched. I can only protect you when you're hiding."

"What about money? How will I pay my mortgage if I'm not working?"

"It's covered."

"Covered?"

"Yes."

Oh, God, not this again. "Explain."

"I'll cover all of your expenses."

"How?"

"With money."

"You're being difficult."

"So are you." His hands strangled the steering wheel.

I needed more time to plan a strategy. He must have a weakness. I could trick him . . . possibly. I could hit him with a bat again. No, I'd feel bad. Sex? No, he'd just take me to the hiding place for more.

"Take me home first. I have to pack."

"Everything can be bought for now."

I huffed, crossing my arms, jerking his handcuffed arm toward me. "How long will this take?"

"Maybe a couple of days . . . maybe a couple of years."

My mouth fell open. He couldn't be serious. Locked up somewhere for a couple of years?

Brett's finger glided across my bottom lip. "It could be a lot of fun."

"Not on your life!" I fumed. "If you're going to kidnap me then you don't get any fun."

Brett just smiled.

"I'm hungry." I said. "I'm going to pass out unless you feed me."

"I'll stop at a drive-thru."

"Fine with me." I wasn't going to argue with him about food. I already foresaw many other arguments in my future.

Brett ordered a double cheeseburger with fries and a giant soda for me.

"Wait," I said, leaning over Brett to talk into the speaker. "I also want fried cheese curds and two pies."

"If you keep leaning over me like that, I'm going to let you order all the time," he said pulling to the window to pay.

I ignored him, grabbed the bag, and stuffed my face. Brett watched wide-eyed as I annihilated all the food. I didn't care. No one was going to come between me and my food. Swimsuits be damned. If this is what Kirby felt like when he got the munchies, I may have to be nicer to him.

"I'm going to die," I moaned in agony as I polished off the last pie.

"You ate too much."

"Thank you, Einstein."

He raised a brow.

I had no idea where he was driving. I had lost track while wolfing down the fried cheese curds. We had to be out of Madison. There were farms everywhere I looked. It was nearly five o'clock and both dinners were scheduled to start at six.

Brett turned the car onto a narrow dirt driveway that ended in front of a charming stone house. The lights were on, and a soft glow fell on the porch.

"Where are we?" I asked.

"Home . . . for now."

I opened the car door. "I can't get out of the car when I'm attached to you."

"Hop over to my side."

I remembered my lack of underwear. "You hop over to my side."

"I'll end up crushing you."

"Then uncuff me so I can get out."

"You won't run, will you?"

"I have no idea where we are, and I'm wearing a dress and sandals. It's not an issue."

He uncuffed me, watching me with hawk eyes. I slipped out of the car and stepped toward the house. It was small and cute with mossy stone walls and knotty old trees. I could envision the house hiding in the back hills of a Monet-style landscape.

Brett caught my expression. "Don't fall in love with this place. It's only temporary."

He recognized the look in my eye that said "family." I get that look every once in a while. It normally goes away when I hear screaming children or the latest idiotic stunt a friend's husband has tried to pull.

I toured the inside. The living room was filled with comfortable furniture that faced a stone fireplace. It had a dainty but functional kitchen and one bedroom with a queen-sized bed.

Okay, this wasn't meant for a family. It was meant to make a family. I eyed Brett suspiciously. I couldn't see him wanting to make a family with me, but I'm sure he wouldn't mind going through the motions.

I sensed Brett closing in behind me. He rested both hands on my shoulders and pressed my back against his chest. "I've been waiting to get my hands on you since the day we met."

"Don't tell me this was a ploy to have sex with me."

Brett spun me around to face him. "I don't need a ploy."

He kissed me tenderly. It surprised me. I knew he could be passionate, but tender and loving was something new. My resolve weakened. I slipped my arms around his neck. He scooped me up in his arms, carrying me to the bedroom.

"You're mine tonight." Brett gently put me on the bed. As he moved to slide on top of me, his handcuffs skimmed across my leg and up to my hip. A wicked idea blazed through. I had every intention of being his, but not right now. I ran my hands up his shirt. His muscles contracted as my hand glided over them. Vitality radiated from him.

Time to put my idea into motion. I made a move to roll on top of him and straddle him.

Oh, God, not a good idea.

Sitting on him made concentration and self-control spiral out of control. Why did destiny give me this man to outsmart and outmaneuver? His hands ran up my thigh. Higher and higher. His hands roamed until . . .

"Sweet thing," he moaned.

Oops.

He had moved his hands high enough to figure out I was going commando.

Perfect distraction.

I heisted the cuffs while he explored. I slapped them on him and then on the bed frame. I quickly scurried off. His eyebrows shot up.

"Sorry, I'll be back tonight."

I swiped his keys from the nightstand and ran to the door. The Viper sat waiting for its owner in the driveway.

"You're mine tonight," I told the car. I slammed it in reverse and peeled out.

Nagging guilt did its best to try to force me to turn around. I felt bad for tricking Brett and handcuffing him to the bed, but not bad enough to go back. He'd have done the same thing to me if our roles were reversed. I'll just have to take the punishment when I release him tonight. A silly grin spread across my face.

I turned on a road I recognized. It didn't take me long to find my way to Kym's rehearsal dinner. Everyone was already there. I was late, but not late enough to miss anything.

Kym was sipping a cocktail near Jim when I tapped her on the shoulder.

"Mars!" Kym cried out. "You made it. Brett said you wouldn't, but I knew you'd come." She gave me a bear hug. "Are you feeling better? I was so worried."

"I'm fine now," I assured her.

"What's going on with you and Brett?"

"I have no idea," I said.

Kym eyed me suspiciously.

Kym's mom tapped her on the shoulder. "Father Tom is here. He's ready to start the rehearsal."

We stood in a private dining room for our makeshift rehearsal hall. It was perfect. Everyone could stay in one place, and we didn't have to worry about extra driving between the church and the restaurant.

Jim and Kym stood together, peaceful and happy. They held hands, listening to Father Tom. It wasn't even the wedding day and I was already searching for a tissue in my purse. I was on the brink of dumping out my purse when someone handed me a tissue.

"Thank you," I whispered.

"You're welcome," Brett hissed. I jumped as his breath tickled my ear. He slapped the handcuff back on before I could stop him.

"How did you escape?" I whispered under my breath.

He ignored my question. "Tonight, I'm going to try the same trick on you, but I won't run away."

Uh-oh!

Kym and Jim's rehearsal ended. Everyone found their places for dinner. Brett installed himself next to me, resting his free arm on the back of my chair. His fingers teased the back of my neck. At least he wasn't holding a grudge.

With the copious amount of food I'd inhaled earlier, I wasn't hungry for dinner. I ate a couple of bites and moved some food onto Brett's plate to make it look like I was eating. Brett either didn't notice or didn't care because he ate whatever I gave him.

I heard Kym at the other end of the table talking about their honeymoon plans. Jim had booked a hut on the shore of Tahiti. Kym pulled out a brochure and passed it around for everyone to admire. I stared at the romantic luxury hut next to the azure ocean. Someday, I thought, I'll get the romantic honeymoon. I stopped my thoughts from continuing.

I didn't want to make Brett nervous at my brochure ogling, so I quickly passed the brochure to the lady next to me. His eyes were on me. I ignored the heat of his gaze.

His breath was warm on my neck. "Just say the word and I'll take you there." He placed a soft kiss on my neck.

I turned to him. His eyes were warm and chocolaty. My lips crushed to his. I couldn't even move or breathe. What am I doing?

Brett pulled back, resting his forehead on mine. "Keep doing that and I'll never bring you back."

Kym caught my eye. She had witnessed the whole thing. Her jaw hung open. I flushed and peeked around. No one else seemed to have noticed, or if they did, they'd already looked away.

"Omigod," she mouthed to me.

I shrugged and tried to do a palms up, forgetting Brett was still handcuffed to me. I clothes-lined a wine glass with the cuffs, knocking it into his lap. Red wine soaked his jeans and ran down the sides. I gasped and grabbed for a napkin to dab off the wine. Brett smirked at me as I was about to dab his privates. I threw the napkin at him.

* * *

We ducked out a little early. I wanted to go see the Stevensons' party while it was still happening.

"Brett," I said with extra sugar. "I have to go see the Stevensons' party. You don't even have to let me out of the car, just drive me there."

He sighed. "You obviously don't comprehend the word no. I'll take you there, but you have to promise not to pull anything."

"I promise," I said sweetly. "Anyway, what could I possibly do? I'm still handcuffed to you."

He didn't look convinced.

He parked on the side of the road by a rolling prairie. The tent glowed softly as guests danced to the gentle music.

Flower Power had made wildflower leis and crowns for the guests to wear. Everyone looked like overdressed hippies. I smiled at the sight. Small lanterns lit a path that meandered through the prairie and down to a stream.

Before dinner, the Stevensons had renewed their vows at the edge of the stream. In the event request form, they stated Mr. Stevenson had proposed by a stream in a prairie field.

"Can we go to the stream?" I asked Brett.

He studied my face and caved. "Yes," he said, stepping out of the car. I slipped out after him.

The string quartet's enchanting melody floated from the tent, carrying through the night air.

"Everyone looks like they are having a good time," I said.

I'll have to thank Flower Power. It must have taken an enormous amount of time and love to put all these wildflowers together and create such beautiful pieces. Adding flowers to a table is ordinary; adding flowers to a person is extraordinary.

"There you are," Jocelyn cooed to Brett, grabbing his left arm.

I breathed in a sigh of relief since I was still attached to his right. I didn't want to have to explain the cuffs. Thankfully, she was too focused on Brett's mouth to notice.

"I was going to have to get very mad at Mars if she didn't have you come here tonight." She laughed at her so-called humor. Unfortunately, it was the truth.

"Why don't we take a walk down the path?" Jocelyn urged Brett. Her finger played with a button on his shirt.

Brett looked at me for help. He wasn't going to be patient for much longer, not when he was in cop mode.

"Uh, he can't," I stumbled for an excuse. "He's allergic to the wildflowers out here. He just came by to see the event, but he has to leave now."

"Wonderful!" Jocelyn exclaimed. Her eyes lit up. "Why don't we stop to have a drink?"

Ugh! I didn't foresee that. Brett looked to the sky like he was praying for a miracle.

"He has to go to Longhorn's," I attempted another lie. "He still works there."

Jocelyn deflated a little. "I wasn't planning on going there tonight. I guess I could stop in for a few minutes."

"Perfect," I said. "Why don't you go home and change. You can see Brett later."

Jocelyn winked at Brett before she smacked his ass and sashayed to her car.

Brett looked at me. "I'm not going to Longhorn's. I already quit and there's no way I'm taking you there."

"You quit?"

"I can't protect you and work at the same time. We found that out the hard way," he said, kissing my forehead. "The only reason I started Longhorn's was to find the Hammer, which I did, thanks to you. Now I just have to bait her to come out and show herself."

We strolled, hand in handcuffed hand, down the path. The lanterns let off a warm glow that lit the path.

"How are you going to bait her?"

"She's going to be mad I quit. I'm sure she'll blame you and come looking for you."

"So, I'm the bait?"

"In a way, yes. I didn't want it to happen this way. Are you going to be okay with this?" he asked. "I'm going to stick close to you so she doesn't have a chance to attack."

"If she can't attack, how will you catch her?"

"I'm hoping she'll become desperate and slip up."

"What if you uncuff me and let me bait her?"

"It's not worth the risk." He brushed a finger against my cheek. "If I don't catch her this time, I'll catch her later. I'm not risking your life. You've already used up at least three lives so far."

"What if I'm willing to risk it?"

"Sweet thing, I don't gamble with anyone's life but my own."

We reached the stream. Without the sun's light, the water pooled like black silk. Sounds of water moving gently against small, shiny rocks and the far-off string quartet played in my ear.

"We need to get back to the car," Brett said. His voice had an edge to it, jolting me from the romantic moment. "Someone's out here." He drew a gun that was tucked into the back of his jeans. He placed his hand at the small of my back, steering me quickly back up the path. His eyes scanned the darkness.

I crawled into the car firs and he followed after me. The engine revved to life. Brett floored the car.

"How do you know someone was out there? I didn't see or hear anything."

"She was too far away for you to see or hear." He pulled a tranquilizer dart from his pant leg. He had been shot, but the dart had caught in the loose fabric. "Which is why she missed."

"Are you okay?" I squeaked.

"I'm fine," he gritted.

"How do you know it's the Hammer?"

"The Hammer has used tranquilizers before to stun the victim."

"Why not just shoot them with bullets and get it over with?"

"She's not sane," Brett explained. He sounded calm, but his jaw was clenched. Fierce. "After shooting the victim with a tranquilizer dart, the Hammer abducts the victim to a remote location and waits for them to gain consciousness. She tortures them with initial blows from the sledgehammer. She'll finally kill them with the final blow when they've nearly hemorrhaged to death. The crime scenes are gruesome. The victims are almost always unrecognizable."

I stared blankly out at the empty road before me. My stomach churned.

"Brett, stop the car. I'm going to be sick."

Brett looked over at me and decided I wasn't joking. I opened the door and heaved. My huge dinner erupted from my stomach.

Brett winced and handed me my leftover fast-food soda to rinse my mouth. It was watered down but better than nothing.

Brett slipped out his cell phone. "I need a different car," he said to the person on the other line. "Something that will blend in." Brett was about to hang up the phone. "Hey, T? Make sure it has tinted windows. You know where I am, right?"

"Ow," I whimpered.

Something jabbed me through my purse. I reached in my purse to see what it was. There wasn't anything pokey on the inside. I flipped the purse around.

"Uh-oh."

Brett glanced down, focusing on the dart that had penetrated my purse . . . that I had unwittingly stuck in my leg. I yanked it out with a wince. A spot of blood beaded at the spot.

"Don't worry," Brett said gently. "You'll sleep for a little while and wake up in my arms. I promise, sweet thing"

I placed my hand in his, and he squeezed it reassuringly.

I could see he was talking to me, but my ears stopped listening. I couldn't keep my eyes open any longer.

*   *   *

Brett kept his promise. I awoke to find his arms around me. We were lying on the bed in the little stone house. The bedroom was drenched in sun.

My neck tickled with Brett's sleeping breath. I slipped from his arms and struggled to stand. The tranquilizer left my body heavy and rundown.

I'm getting really sick of people drugging and tranquilizing me, I thought as I was finally able to stand without falling back to the bed.

I looked down to find myself in sweatpants and a T-shirt. Considering I didn't have underwear on last night, Brett must have seen the full showcase. Should I kick him now or later? I glanced down to see his relaxed, sleeping face. He was peaceful. Too peaceful to kick.

I'll do it later.

I picked up Brett's phone from the nightstand to look at the time. There was another text message on the phone. I wasn't sure if I should read it, but he had stripped me down last night. I believe that entitles me to see a message.

You didn't show up last night! We made a deal.

I carefully set the phone back down. With everything that had happened last night, I had forgotten Brett was supposed to meet someone at eleven. He must have brought me back here and stayed with me.

I leaned over the bed, giving him a small kiss above his brow. His arms reached out like tentacles grabbing their prey. He pulled me back into bed.

I stuck my hand between our mouths before he could kiss me. I wiggled to free myself.

He didn't ease his grip. "Kiss me, or I won't let you go."

I gave him a quick peck on the cheek.

"That doesn't count."

"It counts," I said. "You didn't specify what kind of kiss."

"Mars, if you don't kiss me right now, I'll have to skip the kiss and move on to unbelievably mind-blowing sex."

I paused. "You just lay it out on the table, don't you?"

"I don't play games . . . unless you're the prize."

"If I kiss you, will you answer a question for me?"

"Maybe. It depends on the question and how good the kiss is." A devious smile crept on his face.

"Who were you supposed to meet last night at eleven?"

"Hmm . . . to answer that question, the payment would have to be made in the French variety and make it extra dirty."

I glared at him. "You would have made that the payment for any question asked."

"You want to argue or pay up?"

Hell, I'll pay up. I won twice on this deal. A question gets answered, and I kiss Brett. No brainer there.

I moved in closer, our lips parted as they touched gently. I grazed his lips with my tongue. He tightened his hold, pressing me into his firm, bare chest.

I pushed back, trekking down to his stomach, kissing his muscles that swelled under his tan skin. I drew a path with the tip of my tongue back up his chest.

He moaned, grabbing my arms to yank me back up. I brought my mouth down to his. His lips were hard and demanding.

Propping myself up to look in his warm cocoa eyes, I said, "Answer the question. I paid."

He nuzzled into my neck while he answered, "Karina."

My first reaction was to kick him, but instead I asked, "Why?"

"That's another question. I believe the payment for answering that question will be big."

"How big?"

"Give me your shirt."

"I changed my mind. I don't want to know your business with Karina."

"Trust me, you want to know."

"You want my shirt? You'll have to take it."

Brett's lips curled with amusement. I turned to jump off the bed, but his arms wrapped around my waist. I pivoted to escape his grasp and landed on top of him.

His strong hands slid up my back, taking the shirt with it. He stripped it off over my head. Our skin touched, smooth and heated. He rolled over, pinning me down with his weight. I inhaled sharply as he brushed his finger against my nipple. His mouth took possession. His tongue swirled and flicked against the hardness. I moaned as he sucked gently. My back arched from the touch of his lips.

I pushed him back again. It was getting more difficult by the second.

"Talk," I said between breaths.

"T said he could help me get evidence that the Fenwigs were paying for sex and not informing the person that they were being filmed. I could get them on soliciting at the very least. Hopefully it'd stop them and get them off our backs.

"When Karina called and made me an offer, I asked the police for assistance. But it didn't happen. Since you were tranquilized, I didn't want to leave you."

Brett nibbled on my shoulder, his thumb mindlessly stroking. Concentrating was nearly impossible.

"Who is T?"

Brett grinned. "If I had any idea I could get payments like these for answering your questions, I'd have made you pay up on Saturday."

"It wouldn't have worked. I didn't care about you then."

"And you care about me now?" He smirked, eyes assessing.

I sighed. "It's impossible not to."

His lips framed his perfect white teeth. "Pants," he demanded.

"What?"

"That's the next payment." He cast his gaze down.

He didn't wait for a reply. His hands worked quickly to strip off the remainder of my clothes.

I was naked next to him. He gazed at me hungrily but didn't touch. He took in every detail. I made a move to escape his predatory stare. His hand pressed my shoulder back to the bed.

Brett kissed me hard. His mouth slowly wandered down my neck, then to my breasts. He lingered there for a moment, but his tongue was on the move. It traveled down the length of my stomach. He devoured everything he came in contact with. My body ached with need. He held me down firmly, my body vibrating under his touch. His mouth traveled lower and lower and . . .

"OMIGOD!"

* * *

"T is the guy with the tarantula tattoo." Brett whispered in my ear.

I draped on the bed unbelievably satisfied and content after his mouth had performed something that could only be considered supernatural.

"He said he would assist the cops in exchange for reduced parole time," Brett continued.

I didn't care about the questions anymore. I didn't care about anything. Just being in bed with Brett took care of all my needs.

As I lay in the crook of his arm, one question floated down and registered in my brain. "Why would Fenwig hire a convict?"

"Finally," Brett said.

"Finally?"

"I've been waiting for this question," he growled. "Final payment."

Brett rolled on top of me, pinning my wrists down above my head.

He searched my eyes. "All you have to say is no," he said.

I didn't say anything. His eyes lit up with a seductive glow. "I'm going to make you scream my name," he promised.

Chapter 14

Brett made good on his word. So good, in fact, that I screamed his name a half dozen times. I lay on the bed deliriously happy and unable to move. Brett brought me coffee. It's a dangerous thing to do when you're still naked. I looked at him, admiring his ample features that made me never want to leave this bed.

"I'm guessing Fenwig hired T as a sort of bodyguard and driver. If Fenwig had shady deals going on, who better to have at your side than a convict," Brett said.

"Huh?" I shook my head to clear out the Brett-induced coma.

"The answer to your last question."

I smiled. "I forgot."

"That's what I aim for," he said, stealing a kiss. "But it's time to get up."

"Where are we going?"

"The wedding."

"Oh, geez!" I threw back the sheet and scrambled to the bathroom. "I forgot that too. What time is it?"

"A few minutes after twelve."

"I need to be at the salon at one."

"I can get you there by then."

"Where's my dress?"

"Emmy took it to your house. T just went to get it," Brett said.

He watched me frantically circle the room. On my third pass, he caught me and steered me to the shower.

"He'll be here soon. Just take a shower and try to relax."

"But I need other stuff too."

"I told him to bring everything that looked girly."

"And have him bring the white bag that's sitting in the closet. It has my shoes and . . . other stuff."

"Just shower. I'll call him now."

Brett strolled out. I turned on the water and let it roll over me until he came back in and plucked me out.

"Time for you to get out so I can get ready," he said. He wrapped a towel around me, taking my place in the warm shower.

"I was afraid you were going to try and stop me from going to the wedding."

"I was, but you'd never forgive me, and it's easier to say yes to you. But," he warned before I could leave, "I'll be by you at all times."

"I don't mind," I said as I left the bathroom.

My dress was draped on the bed. I slipped it on and let out a relieved sigh when it zipped. It fit snuggly, but my boobs didn't bulge out like an inflatable raft. I still hated the dress. It might suit a Las Vegas wedding, but certainly not Kym's romantic garden ceremony. I unzipped the dress and took it off, placing it back on the bed. Even though I despised it, I didn't want it to get ruined at the salon.

I dumped out a bag that had clothes in it. They were unfamiliar to me. I pulled out a pair of jeans and a T-shirt with the store tags still on.

At least T remembered to pack underwear. Attempting to make the image of T rummaging around through my underwear drawer disappear, I thought of the wedding.

Emmy and Curtis probably split up to tackle the garden and hotel separately. I'm going to owe them big time for all the extra work they've been picking up for me.

Brett opened the bathroom door. My eyes shot over to the towel that hung loosely on his hips. I bit my bottom lip as he walked toward me. As he passed by, I looped my finger in his towel, letting him walk out of it.

The towel fell to the floor.

He turned to look at the towel on the floor and then at me.

"Careful," he warned, "you may not make it to the salon."

I smiled innocently. The naked men I've seen before were not a very exciting sight. I have yet to see a man in a Speedo at the beach and think, "He's hot." Brett was different. He made me want to become a peeping Tom.

"Ready?" he asked.

I blinked as I realized he was already dressed. He shoved his gun in the back waistband of his jeans.

"Yes," I said, eyeing the gun.

Brett's cop persona took over as soon as we hit the driveway. His jaw was rigid. His eyes took in everything. I'd be sorry for anyone who tried to mess with him.

"New car?" I asked as I slid in.

"The Viper is too recognizable."

"This car will blend in. There have to be millions of these cars on the road."

"That was the point."

It wasn't a bad car. It looked reliable like my old car. Speaking of my car. . . "Brett, where's my car?"

"It's at the body shop again."

"How much is it going to cost?" A lump caught in my throat. How am I going to pay for it? Even with insurance, I still had a huge deductible.

"Sweet thing, don't worry about it. I got you into this mess, and I'll get you out."

"But you quit your job."

"I wasn't working at Longhorn's for the money. Of course," he smirked, "it wasn't bad money." He brushed his finger on the ridge of my nose. "You were my best tipper."

My face flushed pink.

"You blushed again."

"I know. Are you independently wealthy?"

"No."

"Drug dealer?"

"No."

"Will you tell me?"

"Wouldn't that kill the mystery?" he teased.

"I'm willing to risk it."

"I've been collecting rewards by turning in wanted fugitives."

"So, you had to hunt them down?"

He nodded.

"Kind of like a bounty hunter?"

He nodded again.

I could see him doing it, but it made me nervous. The fugitives had a reward for their capture for a reason. Brett could be a powerful force, but so could they. And while Brett stayed within the law, they were already beyond that.

"Are you going to be a cop again?"

"Maybe. Right now, I just want to keep you safe and put the Hammer behind bars."

* * *

We stepped into the salon. Brett lingered near the front door, guarding it. I walked over to Kym.

"Hey, good-looking," Kym called to Brett from her salon chair. "What's he doing here?" she whispered to me.

"That psycho killer is still after me. He said he won't let me out of his sight. It was either bring him here or go into hiding."

"Go into hiding with that gorgeous man?" Fran asked, listening in on the conversation.

"Yes, but Kym comes first," I said to appease Kym. "Besides, he is way too much for me. I couldn't imagine being trapped alone with him." I blushed.

Kym raised her eyebrow and lowered her voice. "You had sex with him."

Fran and Kate leaned in to hear.

"I don't know what you are talking about."

"She did," Kym said to Fran and Kate. "She always says that when she is hiding something." Kym turned to me. "Please, tell me it was horrible so I don't get jealous."

"It was completely horrible. He's got looks, but he's got nothing where it counts. He was clumsy and awkward."

Kym huffed. "Damn! I know you're lying. He moved great on the catwalk, and his thong showed he most definitely has it where it counts."

"He stuffs his thong with a sock."

"I know a package when I see one," Kym said. "That was the biggest gift to women ever wrapped in a thong."

We all giggled. Brett looked over at us suspiciously.

The salon had us beautified in record time. Hair, makeup, and nails were done. They gave us all updos, but each of us had a slight variation. They curled my hair into ringlets that fell alongside my face.

"Cute," Brett said as we were leaving. He pulled a curl to see it spring back. "Are we going to the garden now?"

"Yes, please."

"What were you girls talking about?"

"You."

He raised an eyebrow. "You talked about me? Anything I should know about?"

"Hey, if you come into a salon with a bunch of girls, you're going to get talked about. And it's certainly nothing you want to know about."

*　*　*

Emmy met us at the garden parking lot. She led the group to the tent designated for the bride. It wasn't a large tent, but it far exceeded the needs of four women. Brett entered the tent first to search it.

"What's he doing?" Emmy whispered to me.

"Searching the tent," I explained. "He's an ex-cop. Old habits die hard."

"You can say that again. I still bite my nails."

Brett nodded, and we entered.

"Well," Emmy said, "I'll let you get settled in, and then I'll be back to check on you in a half-hour. There's a radio on the table if you need me."

Emmy left and Brett stayed. I tried to push Brett out through the tent flap, but he didn't budge.

"You can't stay here," I told him. "Kym and the rest of us have to change."

"I'm not leaving," he said as I leaned all my weight on him. He didn't budge. "The tent isn't sealed at the bottom. The Hammer could sneak in here quickly and quietly."

"Let him stay," Kym said. "There's a privacy screen we can dress behind." She leaned in to whisper. "Plus, he's great to look at. It'll make Jim jealous to find out there's a hot man in my dressing room."

"You're horrible," I chuckled. "You're not supposed to make the groom jealous on his wedding day."

"It keeps the romance hot. Tonight, I will reap the rewards of my efforts." Kym winked.

I rolled my eyes. "You can stay," I told Brett.

We helped Kym dress first. Her dress formed to her beautifully. The strapless gown was pure white. Swirls of pearls ran throughout the dress and down the train. She perched on a stool once she was all arranged. I fluffed out her dress and train to fall flat so it wouldn't wrinkle.

"You're gorgeous," I told her.

I tried hard to keep the tears from gushing. Of course I was happy for her! But life would be different. Our friendship would be different. Damn it! One little tear escaped.

Brett noticed. He notices everything. He took a tissue from the table and wiped the tear away. I breathed in deeply to suppress a fit of hysterical sobbing by his simple gesture. This was going to be a long day.

Brett bent down to give Kym a small kiss on the cheek. "You look beautiful."

While I composed myself, Kate changed, and then Fran changed. When Fran reappeared, I grabbed my dress and white bag and ducked behind the screen.

Kym looked nervous. "Did you try the dress? Did it fit?"

"I tried it on this morning and it fit. It's still snug, but I'm sure nothing will pop out."

Kym relaxed.

I dug in the bag and pulled out the thigh-high stockings along with garter belts that had orchid-colored roses sewn onto them. Kym said this was in case the guests were treated to a little peek-a-boo from our dresses moving the wrong way. I wasn't going to show them to Brett. I'd never make it to the wedding.

I stepped out from behind the screen. "Well, is it okay?" I asked everyone.

"It fits perfectly," Kym said, clapping her hands. "You look hot."

I looked like an expensive prostitute. But Kym was happy. I guess that's all that matters.

Judging from Brett's expression, a very dirty thought was brewing in his mind. He then dipped behind the privacy screen and reappeared wearing a tailored black suit. His collar was unbuttoned. When Fran saw him, she fanned herself with her hand.

I examined him with the same dirty expression he'd given me.

He smiled. "Do I look that good?"

"You know you do," I said. "You clean up nicely."

Kym let out her best wolf whistle. "Brett, I don't mind swapping out the groom today if you'd be the replacement."

"I'd be at the altar in a heartbeat, but I've already found a girl who's a keeper," he said, giving me a wink.

Emmy peeked into the tent. "Kym, Father Tom said the ceremony should start in five minutes."

Emmy's eye caught on my dress. She opened her mouth to say something, but nothing came out.

"I already know. Don't bother saying anything," I said under my breath.

"Did you ever think you missed your calling in life?" Emmy asked. "I've heard high-class call girls can make a ton of money."

"I'll keep that in mind," I said, guiding her out of the tent.

Brett stood in the corner with an amused expression.

"Are you ready, Kym?" I asked.

"I'm ready."

"You are amazing and beautiful, and Jim is a good guy. He'll make you happy," I said, more for my ears then hers. He already does make her happy. Who's to say what the future holds? "And then you can have babies, and I can be Auntie Mars."

I helped Kym stand and smoothed her dress. Brett took his stance at the door flap to let us out.

"You're not planning to stand next to me during the ceremony are you?"

"No, but I'll be close."

Kym's dad showed up right before the music started to walk her down the aisle. Elephants stampeded in my stomach. Kym, on the other hand, was the picture of relaxation and composure.

Fran walked out of the tent and down the flower path first, followed by Kate. Brett stole a kiss from me as I followed Kate out.

Kym paired me to walk down the aisle with one of Jim's single groomsmen. I had always thought Jim had good taste, but his choice of best man was questionable.

Ed, the best man, who licked his lips when he saw me, is a man I dread being around. When not forced into a tux, he can be found wearing a tattered, sleeveless undershirt and a pair of very unflattering cutoff jean shorts that ride up his hairy, well-fed butt. His favorite saying is: "Get me a beer." Always followed by a monstrous belch.

When I asked Jim how they became friends, the answer he gave was fuzzy at best. He ended up saying you don't pick your friends, they just show up on your doorstep. Needless to say, I wasn't happy about having to walk down the aisle with Ed.

I tried to keep my focus at the end of the aisle and not look at the guests when I passed by them with Ed. From my peripheral vision, I could see wives giving their husbands an elbow to the ribs to close their gaping mouths. Ed was making honking gestures to the amusement of his friends.

I'm sure they were judging me. I wanted to yell, "I didn't pick the dress!"

Jim and his groomsmen smiled as I took my place, but not before Ed slapped my ass. I glared at him. He made a humping motion back at me.

Kym was right, though; the dress was cooler. It made standing in the hot sun almost bearable. Guests fanned themselves with their programs and drank water from water bottles inscribed with Kym and Jim's names and wedding date.

Everyone stood as the music changed. We watched as the bride walked down the aisle with her dad. She was stunning with her shimmering blonde hair and white dress. All eyes were on her. I breathed a sigh of relief as she took center stage.

The ceremony was quick. Father Tom dabbed drips of sweat off his forehead as Kym and Jim kissed, making them husband and wife to a round of applause. They smiled and led the way back down the aisle.

Thankfully, the Hammer didn't make an appearance.

A hand closed around my waist. "It was a pretty ceremony, wasn't it?" I asked Brett.

"I didn't see it."

"You said you were going to stay close? Where did you go?"

"I was here."

"Then how in the world didn't you see it?"

"I didn't see it because I couldn't take my eyes off of you." Brett spun me around to face him. "What do you have on?"

"A dress."

"Underneath your dress."

"Uh, nothing special. Why?"

"Liar," he called my bluff. "The wind blew your dress just enough to see a hint of something I want to investigate."

"Aren't you on the lookout for the Hammer?"

"You're very distracting," he said while tracing my cleavage with his finger.

T and Emmy strolled toward us. Emmy looked like a little porcelain doll next to T. She held his tattooed arm tightly. T and Brett gave a nod to each other.

"Karina said she would give you another go, but it has to be tonight, same time," T said discreetly to Brett.

Brett nodded. "I'll be there."

I halted T before he could leave. "Tell her there's a third."

Brett and T gawked at me.

"No," Brett said, shaking his head. "No way."

"You said you'd look after me. I'm not staying by myself in some strange house."

"There's no way I'm letting you go. I have no idea when the police will move in. I may have to get involved a little more than I want to. Do you understand?"

"Oh yeah, I understand," I simmered. "I understand that you're going to end up in bed with her if the police are slow or back out."

"That's why I can't involve you."

My first reaction came on suddenly. My foot flung out to attack his shin. He grabbed me and spun me around so my back was to his chest.

"You can only kick me in the shin once a lifetime. You've already used your one time."

"Uh, okay," T said and backed away with Emmy. "Brett, just give me a call." He took Emmy's hand as they hurried off.

I wasn't about to go down that easily. I stomped on his foot. He released me, cussing under his breath.

"I'm going with you," I said firmly. "It's not up for discussion."

"You are the most stubborn, difficult, pain-in-the-ass person I've ever met!"

"Right back at you," I huffed.

"You're pouting."

"I'm not pouting. I'm mad."

Brett sighed in defeat. "You are, too." He brought me in for a hug. "You win. You can come."

Good. I had no intention of participating in Karina's sex tapes. If Karina got too close to Brett, I'd attack.

"I don't understand," I said. "Why would the Fenwigs want you anyway? They know you have the sex videos."

"They may try to harass me into handing the videos over, or they may want to get some dirt on me so I don't talk. They don't know I was a cop. They probably expect I'm just like Jesse. Money opens a lot of doors in their world."

"I guess." I untangled myself from Brett's hug. "It looks like it's time for pictures."

I made my way over to join Kym and Jim. They posed as the photographer snapped pictures by the hundreds.

The photographer wore a green fedora hat and purple horn-rimmed glasses. He's known in the community as an eccentric artist. I'm not sure why Kym hired him. He's certainly not the photographer I recommended.

"Okay, time to bring in the bridesmaids and the groomsmen," the photographer shouted.

He sucked in air at the sight of me. He tisked and tittered as he circled around and inspected me.

"Can't you stuff these in more?" He poked at my breasts.

I slapped his hand. "No, I can't! You better just do your job and stop touching me."

"I can't have these things in the shot." He gestured at my girls. "They'll take the focus off the bride."

Good grief!

"Just stand me in back." The truth is, I really didn't want to be in the pictures dressed in this getup anyway.

The photographer moved me around like a mannequin, trying to get me to blend in. I gritted my teeth when he took a light-meter reading on my breasts to make sure they wouldn't cause a hot spot in the photo.

Brett stood on the sidelines, trying his hardest not to laugh.

When the last photo was taken, I tromped past the photographer, holding myself back from pushing him into the rose bush. He stopped me and handed me his business card. A naked woman's silhouette was sprawled across it.

"I'm always looking for nude models."

"I'm not a model."

"True. Your facial features aren't structured, but I can sell the rest of your body to any male entertainment magazine."

"Sell my body?" I fumed.

Brett held my arm, ushering me away before I could kick the nudie photographer.

"You were going to kick him, weren't you?"

"Yes! He wanted me to take a nudie picture."

"I'd buy it."

I couldn't help but crack a smile. "Pervert."

"We have a little while before the reception. Why don't we go find a private area to explore?"

It didn't take a genius to break that code. "No, I need to be here for Kym. Besides, it's too hot for that."

"I want to see what you have under that dress." Brett pulled the hem of the dress up a couple of inches. "Shit." He dropped the dress. "I wish I hadn't seen that."

"You don't like them?"

"Them? You have two?"

I nodded.

He groaned. "At least I have the rest of the day to come up with a plan to get them off you."

Something to look forward to.

"Looks like it's time to go."

Kym didn't want her reception in the garden. She wanted to make sure there was air-conditioning and proper plumbing. I completely agreed with her on those points. Especially since this dress was starting to cling to the beads of sweat forming on my skin.

Brett drove us to the hotel where the reception was being held.

"Don't let me drink more than one glass of champagne," I told him.

"I don't seem to be able to stop you from doing much."

"You'll have to do your best. Champagne goes right to my head. If I drink anything else with it, I'll start puking."

"Duly noted."

Emmy and Curtis greeted guests at the main entrance and pointed them in the direction of the ballroom.

Curtis elbowed Emmy when I arrived. He wasn't at the wedding, so he hadn't seen me yet.

"It's not polite to stare," I scolded as Brett and I walked past. It didn't stop him.

The ballroom was lovely. The champagne favors were sitting on the table, labels faced to the front. Candles flickered on each table. Gifts were already piled on the designated table.

My gift to Kym was still sitting at home. I'll have to give it to her later when I'm allowed to go back home. I sighed. It's only been a couple of nights, but I miss my home.

The string quartet from the Stevensons' party was there and already playing. They would play through dinner. The Swinging Aces band would take over for the rest of the night.

"I have to sit at the head table for dinner," I told Brett. "Where are you going to be?"

"Standing at the ballroom doors. T will sit by the emergency exit doors."

"But you have to eat too."

"I already know what's on my menu for the night, sweet thing," he said, playing with the strap on my dress.

* * *

I was good and drank water for most of the evening. I sipped my one glass of champagne cautiously, even though family and friends kept popping up out of their seats like groundhogs to toast the happy couple.

I had to swat Ed's straying hand multiple times as he reached under the table for my thigh. And once he got a little farther than my thigh, I snatched my fork to take a stab at his hand. I missed, but he didn't touch me again after that.

The Swinging Aces started playing. A small scattering of people were on the dance floor getting their groove on—or whatever it's called when your arms and legs betray you. Once the booze kicked in, the dance floor would start pulsating with drunken aunts, uncles, cousins, grandmas, and grandpas.

Most of the family had booked rooms at the hotel, so I didn't need to worry about drunk drivers. Figuring I'd be alone at the wedding, I had even booked a hotel room so I didn't have to worry about driving home.

Emmy had passed out the room keys toward the end of dinner. I took mine and hid it in my stocking. I wasn't going to tell Brett about the room. He'd have whisked me up there before I could finish my dinner.

Speaking of dinner, I hoped he had eaten something. He had been standing at the door during the whole dinner. In between my battles with Ed my eyes had kept straying over to look at him, but he was always occupied. His eyes were narrow, scanning people as they came and left, and even if they were just passing by the door.

I touched the back of Brett's arm. "Are you hungry?"

His face was set. He was in cop mode. "I'll eat later."

"You're not on duty. This is a party."

"I'll be fine."

"Do you want to eat at the bar? There aren't too many people in there."

"Go enjoy yourself, sweet thing. I'll come find you at ten thirty so we can head to Fenwig's."

"You'll eat then?"

"After."

I bit my nail. "You could have room service in my room."

"You have a room here?"

"Yes. Had I known I was going to be here with you, I never would have booked it."

"You're not afraid to be alone with me, are you?" He smirked.

"Only if there is a bed involved."

"Where's the key? You don't have any pockets, and it's not in your hands."

I didn't say anything. His hand flew to my back, steering me to the elevator. Uh-oh!

"Wait. I have to check on Kym."

"She's dancing with her husband right now. They look cute; don't disturb them."

I tapped my foot in the elevator.

"Nervous?"

"You make me nervous."

Brett seized the opportunity and slipped the dress strap off my shoulder. He lowered his mouth to kiss the hollow of my neck and shoulders. The elevator opened.

"After you," he said.

"Maybe this isn't a good idea," I said, sliding the strap back into place.

"I want to see what you're wearing under that dress."

"You already saw."

"Not everything." Brett swooped me up, carrying me to the door. "Open it."

I slid the card out of my stocking and into the card reader. The little light turned green. Brett turned the handle and carried me in.

He stood me on the floor in the middle of the room and then lounged in a chair. "Take it off."

"No," I said. "You have to order room service."

Brett's eyes darkened. Mine widened. I had forgotten how much he loves a challenge.

"Come here."

"No."

"You're being stubborn again."

"I'm only being stubborn because you are."

"If I call room service, will you come here?"

"Yes."

Brett picked up the phone and placed an order for food and a bottle of champagne.

"I've already had a glass of champagne. Anymore and I'll get drunk."

"It's a risk I'm willing to take. Now, come over here."

I moved in close to him.

"Unzip it."

I did, slowly. Brett tugged on the hem, letting the dress fall to my feet.

He groaned. He looped his arms around my legs. His teeth bit into the garter belt to make it snap.

"I always assumed I'd die by taking a bullet during a bust, but I had it wrong. You are going to be the death of me. Since I met you, you've had me running on nonstop high gear."

I sat down on his lap. My fingers carelessly played with the rugged stubble on his face. His eyes were velvety smooth. I kissed him under his jaw and down to his neck.

A knock on the door jolted me back to reality.

"Room service," a female voice announced from the other side of the door.

Already? I grabbed my dress and ran into the bathroom to put it back on. Damn Brett. He gets me so wound up.

I zipped the dress, briefly looked at my reflection in the mirror, and returned to the room.

The room service attendant was standing by the table with her back to me.

"The service here is really fast," I said.

The woman turned around and smiled.

"Annie?" I asked. "I didn't know you worked here."

"It's only temporary," she said.

"Brett, can you believe it's Annie?" I peeked around Annie. His head was slumped over. "Brett?"

"Brett's sleeping right now," Annie said.

"How is he sleeping? He was just awake. He opened the door for you." I looked to see if I could see any movement from Brett.

"I stunned him," she stated. "Just like I'm going to do to you." A smile flashed as her eyes glinted.

Chapter 15

My eyes snapped to Annie. It looked like Annie, the bartender, but somewhere inside her something was broken. Her eyes were wild, her skin was white and taught, and her lips created a violent sneer.

"Why are you doing this?" I asked, backing up.

"You stole him," she snarled. "I warned you to back off. He's mine."

Annie lunged at me with the stun gun. It grazed my arm for a split second. I fell to the ground, dazed but not knocked out. I rubbed the spot that she had zapped.

"You can't get us out of here without people noticing. Just give up and leave us alone," I said as my head buzzed from the electric jolt.

"I don't need to get you out of here," she said. Her lips curved into an eerie smile.

Annie threw the tablecloth off the serving cart to reveal a sledge-hammer. Her hand seized it, dragging it to her.

"I'll scream. People will hear."

"You think I'm stupid, huh?" Annie cackled. "You think I've been dodging cops this whole time by pure luck?"

My eyes focused on Brett.

"Yeah, I knew he was a cop. But as soon as he stepped on the dance floor, I knew he was meant for me. I made him turn from a cop into a dancer."

"Is that when you turned from Jesse to Brett?" My eyes flicked around the room searching for weapons.

"What do you know of Jesse?" she spit out.

"I know what I heard between you and Karina."

"She's a fool." Annie paced the room. She kept her twitching eye on me. "Jesse was mine, but then Brett showed up. Brett's better than any of them. Jesse made a mess of everything. He was arrogant and used his body for money. He had to be put down."

"You killed him?"

"I don't kill men, just whores like you."

"Then who killed him?"

Annie yanked the sledgehammer and smacked it in her hand. "It doesn't really matter. None of it will change your fate."

"Please, let us go," I begged.

"Brett's mine!" Annie stepped closer. "Oh, I'll let you go. Hell is waiting for sluts like you, but I'm going to have a little fun with you first."

"Help!" I screamed. "Someone please help!"

"I told you, I'm not stupid. This floor has been marked for renovation starting on Monday. They don't have anyone booked on this floor . . . except you." She let out a low, fierce laugh. "So, go ahead and scream. No one will hear you. Just imagine the mess they'll have to clean up on Monday," she taunted me. "Your face will be smashed in and they'll wonder who you could be. Brett will forget about you. When he wakes up, I'll tell him you ran away with the EMT. He'll believe that."

Annie paced in front of me. The sledgehammer swung in her hand. "I saw the way that EMT looked at you. You already had him, but you didn't stop there. You had to dig your claws into Brett." Her anger grew with each pass.

"I didn't. Please let me go!" I eyed Brett for any sign of movement.

"You should have died with the drugs I mixed into your mai tai. He saved you. They both saved you!"

"No, the woman with the crazy hair drugged me."

Annie stopped pacing. She snatched my hair, wrapping it around her hand. She yanked my head back, glaring into my eyes.

"Who do you think paid her to do it?" She pulled on my hair with such force that the muscles in my neck strained. "Why do you think I left your glass on the bar while I went to the back to get juice? I added more in because of your slut outfit." She slammed my head against the wall, releasing my hair.

I winced as my head throbbed with blinding pain.

Annie slid her eyes to me. Her face was pinched with hatred. "I'm glad you didn't die from the drugs. It was a misjudgment on my part. Why would I want to kill you so easily, without the added pain and suffering you deserve?" Her eye twitched. The sledgehammer no longer swung down by her legs. She hoisted it up.

"No!"

Annie swung the hammer. I dodged as it crushed the wall behind me. Drywall crumbled on me.

"Don't do this, Annie." I desperately tried to think of anything that would keep her talking and not swinging. "You already killed Brett's sister. If you kill me too, he'll hate you forever."

"She could have been my bridesmaid at our wedding, but she was a slut and had to be punished."

I racked my brain for a way to stall her. "I can help you plan your wedding to Brett. It will be magical. You'll be the prettiest bride ever." I cringed, she can't be buying this.

Annie stopped a moment to look longingly at Brett. He was still slumped over in the chair. I dashed for the door. Annie spun around before I could reach it. She lunged, smashing the door handle clean off. There was no escape.

"I–I was just going to get my event book," I lied. "I could show you samples."

"Enough!" Annie yelled. "I'm going to enjoy killing you more than the others."

Annie swung at me with the hammer. I leapt and threw myself to the other side. The hammer crashed down on the bedside lamp. She spun around and attacked again. I ducked, feeling the breeze of the hammer pass my head. I kept low and rammed myself into her. It knocked her off balance. I flung myself on her, wrapping my arms and legs around her to keep her from using the hammer.

"Get off!" she screeched.

Annie dropped the hammer in the struggle. I could barely keep a hold of her. She smashed us into the wall, loosening my grip. She rammed us again. My back hit the wall. The air whooshed from my lungs, and I crumpled to the floor. I tried to catch my breath, lungs burning with the loss.

Annie strolled across the room as I wheezed. She plucked the sledgehammer from the floor and let it swing near her legs as she advanced. She stood above me, raising the hammer to strike. I couldn't move or scream. I watched as the hammer slammed down toward me.

"I love you," Brett slurred.

I blinked as the hammer stopped an inch from my head. Annie turned to Brett. She blocked my view. I gasped for air.

"Annie, I love you," Brett said, groggily. "I only used Mars to make you jealous. You're the only one I really love."

Annie hesitated but then lowered the hammer and took a step toward Brett. He was still sitting in the chair. His eyes were unfocused as he struggled to regain consciousness. I had to act quickly.

"But you call her pet names, and you protected her from me," Annie said, confused.

"I only did that to protect you. I don't want my future wife to be a murderer anymore."

"Wife?" she asked in a slightly happy, delusional voice.

I crawled to the wall, pulling myself up to lean against it.

"Of course," Brett said. "We can get married tomorrow if you want."

"Oh, Bre…"

Thud.

I stood over Annie with her stun gun in my hand.

"Took you long enough," Brett said.

"Took me long enough? While you were sleeping, she nearly scrambled my brains!"

Brett stood to lumber the few steps to me. I could tell it took a lot of effort. I softened. He grabbed me, pulling me into his arms.

"When I said I love you, it was meant for you," Brett whispered in my ear.

I stared at him in shock. My heart must have been shocked too because it stopped in beating. Brett loves me? I never imagined I'd hear those words from his lips. Maybe he was zapped too hard by the stun gun.

Brett let me go, not asking for the same declaration. He snatched his cuffs from the back waistband of his pants. Annie was still unconscious when he snapped the handcuffs on her. His face was stone as he looked at her. I couldn't read him.

Brett reached into his pocket and grabbed his cell phone to call T.

"Hey, I have the Hammer in cuffs. Come up and babysit," Brett said. "Oh, and I'll slip the key under the door. The door knob in here is busted." He hung up.

"Why does T need to watch her? Can't you just call the police to pick her up?"

"I could, but I won't. I'm transporting her back to Texas." He could tell that I still didn't understand. "I made a promise to my parents."

I nodded.

T made it to the room in good time. He left Emmy down in the ballroom to keep an eye on the reception.

He looked down at Annie as he entered. "I can't believe you fucking caught her. She don't look like much," he said to Brett.

"I didn't. Mars was the one who stunned her."

"Not bad, shorty," he said with a grin that warmed his otherwise scary persona.

"Can you watch her until I get back?"

"Yeah, sure. Just leave the stun gun."

Brett tossed the stun gun to T and grabbed my hand. I snatched the champagne bottle as we left the room. Forget my rule. I've earned a good sloshing with champagne.

In the elevator, Brett dusted the drywall off me. He lingered in certain areas. I took a large gulp of champagne. It fizzed on the way down.

"Where are we going?" I asked.

"We still have a date at eleven."

"We're still going?"

"You don't think a serial killer is going to stop me?"

"I keep forgetting you're not normal."

"The police will meet us a few blocks away from their house."

"You got all the drywall off me, didn't you?"

He inspected me. "Yes, and you're still looking hot."

I didn't feel hot, but I smiled anyway and took another gulp.

"How are you getting T to help you with Annie?"

"Professional courtesy."

I stared him down. "Professional courtesy, my ass."

"What if I said a percentage of the reward for turning her in?"

"Better. I at least believe that."

Brett and I walked through the lobby to get to the parking lot. Jocelyn stood in the lobby with her arms crossed. She wasn't happy about something. She turned and saw us. Her eyes narrowed to slits. Brett wrapped his arm around my shoulder, ushering me past her and out the door. I had a nasty feeling she was going to make my life hell for the next year.

"I thought I was going to have to steer you away from the party," Brett said.

"I'm a little partied out."

"You don't have to go with me. You could stay here or with the police on-site."

"I want to go." I was already so far deep into this I'd need a crane to pull me out.

Brett pulled a limp curl in my hair.

"When will you leave to take Annie back?"

"You're going to miss me, aren't you?" he teased.

"No," I lied. "It'll be a nice break. Kind of like a vacation from the loony bin."

He smiled. "I'm hurt."

This could very well be our last night together, forever. I wasn't sure he would come back once he returned home to Texas. Why would he?

But he did say he loved me, didn't he? I tried to replay the scene in my mind, but I couldn't remember it. It was like it had never happened. Even the parts with Annie swinging at me were clouded and foggy.

I shook my head to clear it.

"You didn't answer my question," I said.

"I'm going to leave as soon as I'm done at Fenwig's," he said. He studied my expression. "I'm sorry. I didn't want to leave this abruptly, but I need to get her back right away."

"I understand," I reassured him. I did understand, but it didn't answer my lingering question about when, or if, he was going to return. I didn't ask. I was afraid of the answer.

Chapter 16

The police were ready and waiting for our arrival. They wired Brett right away. For me, they brought in a female officer to help. The men were leery about me slapping a lawsuit on them for feeling me up while wiring, especially since my dress left hardly any area for the wire to be strategically placed.

"Don't worry," said the female officer. "I've had to do this on myself several times. I found out the hard way what works and what doesn't."

"I've never done anything like this before."

"It's all about acting the part. Just take Brett's lead and follow along."

"You'll come and rescue us though, right?"

"We'll come in as soon as we hear anything incriminating."

I nodded. The bubbles from the champagne were finding their way to my head. The female officer was starting to blur.

Brett came over to fetch me. "Ready?"

"As ready as I'll ever be."

We drove the couple of blocks to Fenwig's house.

It was an impressive two-story, sprawling white house with four pillars in the front. Spotlights shone on the house to increase the awe factor.

Brett rang the doorbell while I took a deep breath.

Karina swung the door wide open. She wore a silk robe loosely tied in the front. I was afraid to know what was underneath. Probably nothing. A sick feeling crawled through me.

She gave Brett a wolfish smile but froze when she caught a glimpse of me.

"What's she doing here? We had a deal."

"Consider it two for the price of one. You won't be sorry."

She took in the full length of me. I tried to act nonchalant, like this was a very normal, everyday occurrence.

"I'm not really into this sort of thing," she said. "But she can come in. It's my money, so I call the shots."

It worked? Karina was actually going to let me in. She also brought up the money. The police should be able to act on that, right?

She led the way upstairs.

"Oh, we're going upstairs," I said, hoping it wasn't too obvious that I was trying to give the police a clue as to where to find us. "What a lovely home you have. This vase in the east wing is gorgeous. Is it an antique?"

Karina gave me a drab history of it, but I couldn't pay attention to anything other than my pounding heartbeat.

Karina led us into a large bedroom. Everything was white—the walls, the carpeting, the furniture, the king-sized bed—it was all white.

I turned to leave, but Brett held me firmly. "Nothing will happen," he whispered.

Think! I scolded myself. "What a lovely bedroom. It's . . . white . . . and having a southern exposure is probably nice in the mornings."

Brett smirked. Karina didn't say anything.

She poured some brandy from her cabinet and gave a glass to each of us. I slammed it, setting the empty glass on the white nightstand.

My eye traveled to the closet door. It was closed. Why is it closed? Fenwig should be in there.

A bad notion crept into my mind. What if they're doing this to make us look like fools? It'd ruin any credibility that we have.

"I bet you have a great walk-in closet," I said to Karina. "Would you mind if I take a look?"

"Feel free," she said. She was too busy circling Brett like a shark to care about me. I slowly opened the closet door. I knew Mayor Fenwig wasn't in there, but it didn't stop the image of him jumping out at me like a troll with his camera.

The closet was enormous. I'd never seen anything like it before. It had to be the size of my bedroom. Expensive built-in wood shelves and cabinets lined the walls. Every nook was filled with designer clothes. A revolving shoe carousel made me shiver with longing. There was even enough room for a chaise lounge, three-way mirror, and a liquor cabinet.

Karina must love her liquor. I imagine being married to Mayor Fenwig is bound to make a person become an alcoholic.

"Don't mind if I do," I said to the bottle of Jack.

I grabbed the bottle and ambled out of the closet. I stopped short at the sight of Karina pawing at Brett like a cat. I chugged Jack. He burned on the way down. It was going to take some serious alcohol to get that image out of my head.

Where the hell are the cops?

Brett looked at me for any sign of Mayor Fenwig or a camera. I shook my head.

Karina was becoming more aggressive. She wasn't going to slow down. I had to find evidence fast.

"Meow."

I stopped in my tracks and turned.

"I'm a bad kitty," she mewled.

My stomach took a belly flop. I couldn't watch. Jack and I continued exploring. Karina didn't take any notice of me. Her eyes were glued to Brett's chest as she unbuttoned his shirt, clawing at him.

Jack, don't fail me now, I thought as I chugged more.

Everything in the room was white. Everything blended together like a stormy blizzard. Cameras, however, are not normally white.

Jack interfered. He was making me gooey inside. Like a sea of . . . goo, swelling in my stomach.

Karina ripped Brett's shirt clean off. He was doing his best to keep her at bay, but she was already going for his pants next.

I turned to set Jack down to help Brett. I had no idea what I was going to do. Sometimes you can over plan these things. Jack, however, had his own agenda and didn't quite make it to the table. The bottle fell to the floor. The thick white carpeting broke the fall. It sucked up the liquid faster than a dehydrated camel.

"When did you last water this thing?" I asked Karina.

Karina pried her eyes away from Brett long enough to see what I was talking about. Her expression changed to horror when she realized the bottle of Jack was sideways on the floor, spilling its contents into her expensive carpeting. Her eyes bugged.

"You clumsy bitch!" she screeched.

Karina snatched the bottle from the floor and slammed it on the table next to a wooden box.

It was a pretty box, but nothing too special. There had to be some reason it was in this white room, being that it wasn't white. I contemplated the box while Karina frantically dabbed the carpet with a white towel.

A circle pattern was carved into the box. One of the circles didn't quite fit in the pattern. I touched it.

"Karina?"

"I'm cleaning up your mess! What do you want?"

"Why is there a camera in this box? Are you filming us?"

Karina stopped dabbing.

Brett opened the box and we both peered in.

"Looks like a camera to me," Brett said.

I turned to Karina. "Did you kill Jesse Corbin? I heard he was a jerk, but I'm pretty sure he didn't deserve to die."

She started dabbing again. "I didn't kill anyone."

"We have the sex videos," Brett said. "We already know what you and your husband were up to."

"It was all consensual, just like it is with us."

"I didn't consent to being taped and neither did Jesse. I bet he was going to use this to his advantage," Brett said, slipping the memory card from his pocket.

Karina chugged down the remaining bit of Jack still in the bottle.

"He was going to blackmail you, wasn't he?" Brett asked.

Karina glared at Brett. "He tried to blackmail us. He was going to take the video and put it on the Internet. It'd have ruined us. My husband was going to fix everything. He said it would go away."

"So your husband killed him?" I asked. "Why did he use a sledgehammer? A gun would've been easier."

Brett looked at Karina. "No, Mayor Fenwig didn't kill Jesse. She killed him. Didn't you?"

She bristled, but a single tear escaped.

Brett continued, "Jesse was going to ruin you. He was going to make sure you suffered."

"You don't understand. Jesse said he loved me. I believed him. I was going to leave Fenwig for him." She broke into a sob. "But then he found the camera. He was going to take everything away from us."

"So you killed him."

"It wasn't like that." Karina grabbed at a tissue. Mascara streamed down her face. "I went to Longhorn's to find him . . . to try to talk to him. He was so angry and unreasonable. He told me he hated me. He said he would make sure that my husband and I ended up in jail."

Brett looked at her in silence. She was lost somewhere deep in her mind.

"I tried to explain," she said bitterly. "He wouldn't even listen to me. He kept saying that he already took precautionary measures and gave the video to someone else. He said that he was going to make a lot of money off me. Annie overhead the conversation." Karina shuddered. "She's insane. She said she knew of a way that I could get him to stop. She told me about the Sledgehammer Killer and how I could kill Jesse. I wouldn't even be a suspect. I told her she was out of her mind. I don't go around killing people."

"Why would she care if you were going to be blackmailed?" Brett asked.

"She doesn't care about me. She wanted to get rid of Jesse. In exchange for his death, she'd find other willing dancers for me. She said anyone except you."

"So you killed him for other men?" I asked.

"No way! I can find men on my own. I told her that she needed help. There was no way I would ever do it. I was even going to go to the police and report her, but then I thought about what she could tell them too. She knew all of my problems. I was so angry at Jesse, I brought the sledgehammer to scare him. I just wanted him to stop." Karina looked up with cold eyes. "He didn't stop. He said I could go to hell. He called me the devil's bitch and that he was going to enjoy watching me suffer," Karina said. Her eyes glazed.

"He shouldn't have said that to you," Brett said, stroking Karina's hair. "It will feel better to let it all out."

She clung to Brett, her shoulders drooped. "I swung."

"What happened, honey?" Brett asked, soothing.

"He dropped lifelessly in front of me. I was so scared, I ran." She sobbed and curled into Brett.

After a few moments, Brett spoke to Karina. "Why did you involve us?"

"My husband and I didn't know what else to do. He thought you might be greedy like Jesse. We hoped we could bribe you to get the videos back, and if that didn't work, we'd try to blackmail you," she said. "It turned into a fiasco. We didn't want to hurt anyone. We were just trying to scare you so you'd give us the videos and leave us alone."

The goo bubbled in my stomach. I heave-hoed onto the carpeting where Karina had dabbed out the Jack puddle.

Brett looked down at my mess. "Nice aim."

"You may want to rethink white," I groaned.

"I don't think she'll have to worry about it," Brett said. "Not for a while at least."

Karina grimaced at the floor but didn't bother to clean it.

The police entered the room and placed Karina under arrest. She sat handcuffed on the bed while they read her her rights.

The police searched for Mayor Fenwig but couldn't find him.

After going over a few details with the police, Brett and I walked to the car.

"You were awesome in there," Brett said.

"You can thank Jack."

"Did you ever think about becoming a cop?"

"Absolutely not."

He was silent for a couple of minutes until he finally said, "I need to take you home. I have to head out."

"Okay," I agreed. "Brett, since they didn't find Mayor Fenwig, do you think they'll let him off the hook?"

"I'm sure the police will do a thorough investigation, but the way I see it, Karina will take the fall. Fenwig may get a slap on the wrist, but he can deny almost all of it. He'll divorce Karina to save public face."

"Will he come after me again?"

"No, there'll be too much publicity on this case. He'll want to lie low."

Brett pulled into my driveway. It felt good to be home but a little lonely too.

Brett escorted me to the door and followed me inside.

"Don't you have to go?" I asked.

"Yes, but I'm going to install your washer and dryer first."

"You don't have to. I know it will be a long night for you."

"I promised I would install them. It will only take me ten minutes. I can't leave you here without any clothes." He smirked. "I already had the pleasure of seeing you in your last outfit. I can't imagine what you'll be parading around in next, and I don't want any other men to see that."

"I don't go parading around," I said. "Don't worry about it. I can get someone else to do it."

"Don't argue. Just let me do this."

Brett's phone rang. "It's T. I'll take the call downstairs." He gave me a kiss on the forehead, shutting the basement door behind him.

A warm draft blew through the living room. I must have left a window open. The front windows were all closed. I looked over to the side living room window. It was wide open. I cursed myself for leaving the window open while having the air-conditioning running. This was going to cost me a fortune.

I shut the window and dragged myself upstairs. I heard a pounding noise behind me. Brett must have already started working on the washer and dryer.

I turned the shower on to get the warm water flowing. I then went into my room to strip off my dress and find some pajamas. The door closed behind me.

"You thought you could get away from me, didn't you?" a ragged voice snarled.

I snapped around to see Annie lock the bedroom door from the inside. "Just in case Brett escapes from the basement, he'll have to knock down two doors to rescue you. By that time, you'll already be dead."

Annie didn't waste any time. She hauled up her sledgehammer.

My heart plummeted to my feet. I had barely escaped her last time; how am I going to get her away from the door?

Annie wildly swung the hammer at me and missed. She was having problems wielding the hammer. There was something wrong.

"How did you get away from T?" I asked, stepping closer to the bat that was resting against the wall.

"It was easy," she bragged. "I tricked him into helping me stand. Poor, helpless Annie with a silly pair of handcuffs," she scoffed. "I grabbed the stun gun when he bent to lift me. I stunned the big oaf before he knew what happened."

Annie's eyes blackened. She moved to swing at me. I jumped on the bed before the hammer smashed into the dresser. She howled in pain.

"Just give up. You're not in any shape to kill me," I said.

"Give up?" She cackled. "You'll never escape the Hammer." She took another swing.

I bounded off the bed away from her.

"Getting tired?" she taunted.

I was tired the first time.

Somewhere in the house a gun fired several times. Annie froze momentarily. I made a dash for the bat. She bolted after me.

I snatched the bat, throwing myself clear of the hammer as she crashed it into the door. Annie unwedged the hammer and turned to strike again. I swung the bat, putting all my weight into it. She buckled to the floor as the bat connected with her stomach. Annie wheezed.

"Feeling a little winded?" I threw back at her.

Brett's hand reached through the hole in the door and unlocked it. He flung it open, aiming his gun at Annie's head, his finger tight against the trigger. I shivered at his anger.

"Brett?" I lightly touched his arm.

His face cleared and he exhaled a long breath. "Cuff her," he said, tossing me handcuffs.

I cuffed her. She groaned in pain.

"How did you get out of your cuffs?" I asked her. "Brett has the keys."

"I pried my hands through." A smile slithered to her face. "I heard the bones snap as they broke."

I shuddered. "How could you have possibly picked up the hammer?"

"The thought of killing you made me enjoy the agony."

Brett pulled me away from her. "Go down to the car and get the shackles from the trunk."

I grabbed the keys and ran outside. As I gathered the shackles, Mrs. J. called to me from across the road. I waved and she hurried across the street.

"I heard gunshots."

"Everything is okay, Mrs. J."

"Who are those for?" Mrs. Janowski pointed to the shackles. "I heard about young people and their kinky sex. Never got into it myself, but I might try. Seems to me like metal shouldn't be in the bedroom though."

"Someone broke into my house. Brett is taking her to the police."

"A woman? You don't say!" Mrs. Janowski looked as happy as punch. "In my day it was only the men who did things like that. I guess that's why people say it's now an equal-opportunity world."

"I guess it might apply to criminals too." I headed to my door. "I need to get these up to Brett."

"Ten four! I'll be standing guard tonight with ol' Bessie. You can rest easy."

"Thanks. If you see any crazy women around my house, just start shooting," I teased.

"Roger that!" she said, hurrying back to her house.

I ran upstairs and handed the shackles to Brett.

"I'll fucking kill you," Annie roared at me. Her face distorted with hatred. "I'll escape again and hunt you down. You better run, bitch."

Seeing her locked up and a gun pointed at her gave me a tiny spark of vigor.

I knelt down and whispered in her ear. "Brett said he loves me. I'm going to marry him and have his babies."

Annie twisted to attack. I quickly moved out of her way. Maybe it wasn't good to provoke a broken mind, but it gave me my strength back. Strength to know she couldn't frighten me again.

"What did you say to her?" Brett looked curiously.

"Girl talk," I said.

Brett escorted Annie down to the car and seat belted her in. She struggled with him. I could see him grasping at his last ounce of restraint. She sunk her teeth into his arm.

"Ow!" he yelled, slamming the door shut. "Do I need to worry about rabies?" he asked.

I shook my head. "She's crazy, not rabid."

Brett smiled before he bent to give me a long, lingering kiss. It was sweet and passionate. I resisted the urge to throw my arms around his neck.

He stepped back. "I'll see you soon, sweet thing."

I nodded.

"You don't believe me, do you?"

I wasn't sure what I believed. I kept quiet.

"Sweet thing, you have to learn to trust me."

He left me with a tender kiss that tingled my lips. I gave him a small wave as he backed out of the driveway and took off down the road.

I sighed and trudged back inside the house. I climbed upstairs to shower and change. As I slipped into my bed, a rapid knock on the front door gave me a jolt.

"Mars, I know you're in there!"

The doorbell buzzed like a furious bee.

"Brett was my territory and you moved in on him. You stole him!"

I peeked out the window. Jocelyn. I knew this was going to bite me in the ass.

I opened the window and called down to her. "Jocelyn, I'm sorry. It just happened. But he's gone now. He left for Texas."

"Nice try! You're fired! Do you hear me? FIRED!"

The rapid sound of ol' Bessie blasted through the night air. Jocelyn screamed as an onslaught of paintballs pelted her. She bolted for her car and peeled out, giving the sniper access to her silver BMW, which was quickly becoming polka-dotted with lime-green paint.

"Thanks, Mrs. J.," I called out.

She gave me a salute.

I fell back into bed. My cell phone chirped. I cringed at the possibility that it might be Jocelyn. I looked at the phone with one eye shut, just in case. It was a text from Evan.

We're going riding tomorrow. I'll pick you up at two.

Even though I was now jobless, I couldn't help but smile. Here we go again.

Keep reading for a sneak peek at the next Mars Cannon novel:

Predator Patrol

Predator Patrol

Preview

I steeled my nerves, puffed out my chest, and held my head high as I walked into The Road Hog Bar. They were looking to hire a bartender, and I was determined to be that person.

I swung open the door with more muscle than I knew I had, slamming the door against the wall. After a moment's pause, I resumed my path to the bar. Eyes followed me. The few patrons that frequented the bar were hardened men and fast women. They all looked like they could use a bath, a shave, and a change of clothing.

These were my customers now, I reminded myself. However scruffy they may be, they're my paycheck.

I flagged down the bartender, who took his time responding. He was in the range of "old man" though I couldn't put a figure on it. He looked as though he'd lived a rough life, so he could be fifty and just look twenty years older, for all I knew. He was gruff, rugged, and could use a bath too.

"I want to apply for the bartending job."

His skeptical eye judged me. His bushy eyebrows drew together. "Go home, kid. This place isn't for you."

"Why not?"

"Look around; then look in a mirror."

"I've looked around. I see a place needing attention. I see a place that could use a good scrub down."

"Let me stop you there. We don't want attention or a good scrub down. Although Bob down there smells a bit off. What I need is a bartender who knows what they're doing and can keep the place in check."

"What do you mean?"

"What would you do if there was a bar fight?"

"Call the cops."

"The cops would be here every week if I called them for every incident. By the time they'd arrive, my bar would be trashed. You have to stop the fight quickly before anyone gets hurt."

"I'm sure I could come up with something. I'm very resourceful."

He shook his head. "I tried hiring a cute lookin' woman before, thinking it'd attract men and keep them at the bar. The first fight she was crying under the tapper, and I was out money for bar repair."

"What if you took me on for a week? Think of it as an apprenticeship. If I can make it a whole week, you hire me."

I'd never fought this hard for a job. I wasn't sure why I didn't just walk out the door and thank the heavens he didn't want me.

His thumb grazed across his coarse stubble. "Go home. It's for your own good." He turned his back as he headed down the bar toward Bob.

"I'll be back tomorrow, old man," I said and strolled out the door.

I'd be back tomorrow. This job is mine. I'm tired of defeat. I'm tired of men walking away. It's my turn to call the shots!

Books by Nicolette Pierce

Mars Cannon Novels
Deadly Dancing
Predator Patrol
Security Squad
Biker Brigade
Fearsome Foursome

Nadia Wolf Novels
The Big Blind
High Stakes
Cashing Out
Squeeze Play
The Last Tailored Suit
My Traitor
Pocketful of Diamonds
Last Hand

Metal Girls Novels
Melting Point
Critical Point
Breaking Point

Loved by Reese
When Rio Surrenders
When Rome Falls
When Edinburgh Dreams
When Sydney Loves
When London Calls

For more information, visit www.NicolettePierce.com.

Made in the USA
Las Vegas, NV
16 November 2020